Devil Up

a novel

by

T.R. Pearson

Barking Mad Press

1879

1

The first one I killed was the first one I ever saw, and I wouldn't have shot him but for his knife and all the whooping. He would have been better off sneaking up and laying my gullet open, but he felt called upon to yip and yell, so I had time to draw a bead. I'd shot plenty of rabbits and probably more than my share of snakes, but it took him to graduate me to Comanches.

I needed a little while afterwards to figure out how I felt. Excited at first—that much I remember—and a little sick about it, but then he kind of woke up, and I had to kill him again. After that, I didn't fret so much and could tell in my bones I was different. I half tried talking it through with Gunther, but he was just a mule.

They tell me I was sixteen years old, so I guess I was

something close to it. Some details are hard to conjure
these days, while others won't leave me alone. I know
Frank was supposed to come with me and a cousin of his
named Calvin, but Frank's daddy got wind of what we
were up to and locked Frank in the cellar. That's what I
heard from Calvin anyway who guessed he'd stay home
too, so on the day we'd planned to set out, just me and
Gunther went.

They didn't any of them think I'd get as far as the Mis-
sissippi. By the time I'd reached the ass end of Kentucky, I
was doubting I'd get there too. Back in those days, it was
hard to go anywhere. There were tracks people traveled,
some of them wide enough for wagons, but there wasn't
much of anything you'd be tempted to call a road. I spent
three solid weeks in the deep woods. That's what it felt like
anyway, and then I reached a few farmsteads and passed
within sight of a couple of puny towns.

You got a sense out there how very big and empty this
country was, and that was even before I'd crossed the
river and made it to the plains. Folks were bunched up
in Paducah and places like that but otherwise scarce on
the ground. Ferrymen could usually tell you the best way
to go, depending on what you were wanting, and one of
them sent me down toward Centralia, which eventually
put me in with the Comanches. That was not a patch of
Oklahoma I'd ever wanted to see.

I'd run into some squaws and grandpa Indians on the
way, but they were all Choctaws or Creeks or something
and were eager to trade for stuff. Sugar mostly and cloth
I'd carried along for that sort of thing. I had a couple of

sacks of brass buttons as well, and they went over big. I swapped out for a buffalo hat I'd eventually be needing against the weather and a bundle of dried elk strips I could eat along the way.

As people go, those Indians were kind of gloomy and dirtier than most like they knew they'd be sleeping on the ground from now on and so couldn't be bothered to bathe. I learned pretty quick they were liars and thieves, but they hardly came off as dangerous and would drop all their conniving once you'd told them you'd had enough.

Comanches were another thing, and most everybody you came across had a story to tell about them. They rode horses, used rifles, and had a natural gift for bloodthirsty wickedness. Worse still, they were said to be thick on the ground where I'd managed to end up. I had a hard time telling just where I was unless I hit a town and could ask. Reading the stars and the map and the compass had been Frank's job, and he was back home. So me and Gunther kept west and just hoped we'd get through the place all right.

Somewhere beyond Enid, I fell in with missionaries. That'd be eight Christian families and a couple of scouts who kept an eye out for threats along the trail. One of the scouts was just a boy like me, and the other was his uncle who drank so much mash it was a going wonder he could stay upright. I kept with those folks for ten or twelve days, and we might have seen a war party once. That's what the drunk scout told us, though it looked to me like buffalo on the horizon. Either way, it was enough to get all those pilgrims prayerful and worked up.

Not that they needed much encouragement. That was a praying gaggle of people, and they let it be known they wouldn't be happy until I was extra Jesusy too, so I put on a show of loving the Lord, but mostly I kept my Colt Navy handy. If savages rode down on us, I doubted Jesus would be much help.

Though maybe He was, at least for a while, because we moved across the open plains largely unmolested. That wouldn't be counting a trio of white men, old Confederates on the prowl, who joined up with us for a couple of days and then helped themselves to a box of scrip, a bundle of harness leather, and three ponies before slipping off in the middle of the night. It was that kind of world out there. You'd left the laws and rules behind.

Those missionaries were aiming to bring the Apache nation to Christ. I don't know how or why they'd settled on that, but they'd all certainly come around to it, and they took to practicing on me even though I was hardly a fit challenge since I'd been raised back in Virginia in a Baptist sort of way.

"Y'all even speak Apache?" I remember asking one of them, and he took the position they didn't much need to.

"The Savior," he told me, "will make a way through."

I decided that night, in consultation with Gunther, that it would probably be sensible for us to go back to traveling alone for a bit.

The next day, I said my goodbyes and broke off on a crossing trail. I didn't much want to be off on my own. The company had been consoling, but I guess I wasn't sufficiently sold on what the Savior could do.

So me and Gunther returned to making our own way,
and I should probably say I never did ride him. He was
packed high with all my prospecting gear, my blankets
and food and my cookpot. I'd walk along ahead of him
with a pouch full of elk and my pistol on my hip. While
we might not have covered a lot of ground from day to
day, we'd move as long as the sun was up and stayed pretty
regular at it. Every now and then we'd find an especially
fetching spot to camp, a shady place near water ordinarily,
and we'd take a day or so off from the grind of marching
across this land.

We'd see coyotes pretty much all the time, jackrabbits
the size of dogs, and every now and then I'd spy buffalo off
and away or feel them running. The ground would shake
a little and there'd be a cloud of dust. Rattlesnakes got so
common I couldn't even be bothered to kill them, and we
had a speckled skunk follow us for nearly a week. I can't
imagine what he was thinking.

I'd been around Gunther for some time by then, so we
knew each other well. I'd worked him on a plow, and he'd
snaked a world of timber. We'd also pulled a wagon with
him in a regular sort of way, so Gunther was about as tame
and broken as a mule can be. Like most mules, though, he
was given to sulks. He wasn't terribly different from people except Gunther in a pout would often ease up behind
me and bite the back of my neck. If that sort of maneuver
wasn't on offer, he'd step on my feet instead.

There aren't many creatures on this earth more expressive than a mule, even if most of what they have to say all
runs in one direction.

So it wasn't like I was lonely for company and needed a batch of missionaries to buck me up and help me cope. Gunther was plenty fine for that, and we had some good times off and alone. Maybe too good and that's why I got a little shiftless. I built a fire one evening and foolishly kept it stoked throughout the night, so my Comanche didn't need to do a lot of work to find me.

If I'd been called upon back then to give advice to Comanche braves, I'd have told those boys to cut down on the whooping. There was nobody better at slipping around and sneaking up on people, but then they'd yip and yell and hoot and cover that final charge out loud. For plenty of folks that was probably too late, but I'm sure there were times when it wasn't. In my case, for instance, I grabbed my Colt and managed to get off a shot.

That fellow was almost on me by then, and he was a hell of a thing to see. He was wearing a topcoat with sateen lapels and a homburg hat with antlers stuck through it. He didn't have a shirt on or proper pants and had run at me with a boot on one foot and something like a spat on the other. They were magpies, those Comanches, they'd kill you and skin you and then dress up in all your stuff.

He was painted too with streaks of yellow and red all over the place, and he was wearing bones and feathers about everywhere he could put them. He hit the ground just shy of me, groaned once, and was still.

I had the good sense to grab Gunther and retire with him into the night just in case there were other Comanches around primed to serve as reinforcements. After I'd held my breath and had listened for a bit to the usual prairie racket, I decided it was safe to go back over and collect my stuff. That's when my Comanche scrambled up and needed shooting again. Like I said, I was sick about it at first but hardened to it soon thereafter.

If every time you got in a tussle out there you chewed over your moral boundaries, there was a going chance some less particular rascal would do you in.

So while I wished I hadn't needed to kill my first Comanche, I used that episode to shift my squeamishness out of the way. I even took his pony with me. She was rigged up in some Indian fashion and had yellow paint on her withers and feathers braided in her mane. I planned on telling people I'd found her loose out on the prairie, which seemed like a thing a greenhorn with a swaybacked mule might do.

I put as much distance as soon as I could between us and that dead brave, even left the trail and cut straight through the scrub. I think I must have veered north a little because after three days of charging hard, I kind of met up with those missionaries again.

I'd found their trail, just strayed across it, and had been on it for some hours when I saw what looked like wagons up ahead. The closer I got, the more I could tell that things weren't as they should be. One of those buckboards was cocked up on its side, and there was no sign of any horses, but I could see blankets and clothes and sacks and mess scattered across the ground.

The drunk scout was the first one I came to. He was sitting up against a barrel and had two arrows in him and a strip of bloody crust where hair had been.

They were all butchered, the men anyway. Shot up, cut up, punctured, scalped, a lot deader than I'd ever seen people. The two women in with them were less torn up but just as dead themselves. By my count, there were five or six women missing and probably as many kids. All the horses were gone and both of the cows. The dogs were still there, but they'd been killed in six or eight ways too.

It was a woeful sight, and the previous me back on the farm in Virginia would have probably run off or dropped to the ground and wept. But prospector me on the open plains who'd shot a man and killed him, just tied a bandana against the stink and had a thorough look around to see if there was anything useful left.

I found a hammer those missionaries wouldn't be needing along with a sack of trail biscuits, a tinderbox, and a couple of canteens. I did say a prayer for all those dead folks as I pulled some boots off of a boy. His name was Daniel, and he had a birthmark that stretched from his cheek to his chin. I remember him telling me about a fish he'd caught that had a fish inside of it.

If I'm honest, I'd even admired his boots back then.

She was watching me all along, wasn't hunkered and hiding at all but was sitting in one of the wagons on a pile of horse tack. It would turn out she'd hid underneath that bunch of reins and bridles and mess while all the war party slaughter was going on.

I yodeled and yelled when I finally saw her in with the wagon clutter, and I could tell by the look on her face she wasn't thinking too highly of me. Poking around. Stealing boots. Seeming all hard and callous.

She was something like ten years old, I think, and was wearing a dress made of sacking. She had one of those haircuts that looked like somebody had given it with a knife. I'd never heard her speak when I was riding with those folks, though I was told she had the gear to do it, and one of the women had informed me the girl was an orphan who'd been conceived in sin.

"You all right?" I asked her.

She didn't say one way or the other but just climbed down from that wagon and grabbed a canteen I'd collected. She drank it about half empty. Then she went hunting a proper shovel. She carried it over to one of the corpses and planted the tip in the ground.

"We can't bury these people." I gave her all my reasons.

She made her unhappy noise. I'd grow familiar with it in time.

"Just can't," I said and kicked at the ground to show how hard it was.

She did a spot of snorting and then held up one finger alone.

"Yeah, all right. Maybe. What one?"

She led me over to the scout. Not the drunk uncle with the arrows but the boy who'd only been about sixteen, like me. He'd gotten shot and stabbed and was covered in blood and dirt, black flies as well.

Him I dug a hole for as best I was able, and then me and the girl both dragged him over, scrunched his parts to make him fit, and covered him up with all the rocks we could find.

I tried to look solemn for a moment and then turned to

walk away, but that girl wouldn't be satisfied until I'd said a few words over him.

"Only knew him a little. Liked him all right. Sad thing he came to this."

She wanted a prayer as well and stood there with her hands together until I'd said the blessing from our supper table every night. She let that be enough, but I could tell she wasn't happy. For a girl who wouldn't speak, she was about as expressive as my mule.

She didn't appear to want to come with me but went straight back to her wagon, climbed up in it and sat pretty much where I'd found her sitting before.

"We ought to leave this place," I told her.

She made one of her noises at me.

"Buzzards and wolves'll be coming soon. Indians might come back."

She stayed right where she was.

"Suit yourself."

I headed over toward Gunther and that Comanche's pony. It was a bluff on my part. I figured she'd climb down and join me once she saw the only other living things heading up the trail.

So I set out thinking she'd follow, but she stayed perched in her wagon, and I stopped up the way to work out what my duty ought to be. I let myself be guided by my having a sister once. She was three years younger than me and died at eight and a half of fever.

I'd been harder on my sister than she'd deserved because I'd figured, like most people, I'd have time later to be decent. That proved enough to send me back to the wagon where that girl was sitting.

I didn't bother talking but just picked her up and hauled her until her squirming and kicking got too much for me. Once I'd turned her loose, she ran into the scrub.

"Do what you want," I told her and went back the way I'd come. I never would have guessed I'd find myself somewhere in Oklahoma with my moody mule, a painted pony I'd taken off a brave I'd killed, and a bloody knot on my leg from getting kicked by a girl. I had a few hard words for Frank and Calvin who'd put me in this fix.

I didn't even look to see where she'd gone until after a couple of hours when I located her off in the scrub following along a good ways back. I think I might have preferred that speckled skunk.

I couldn't tell just what she thought at first, but I got better at it in time. She had her assortment of noises, some faces she'd pull, and the girl knew how to get her way without resorting to a tantrum. She'd make you understand what she wanted, and if you had other ideas, she'd visit on you (for as long as it took) her personal version of "Naw."

It was kind of a squeak, mostly out of her nose, and there was no hope of bargaining with her. For a child conceived in sin, she'd sure arrived with plenty of starch.

Our first night on the plains she was still hanging back until I built enough of a fire to cook us up some beans and jerky. I made her a plate that I set on a rock, and she came up in a while to get it. She stood right there and fed herself while she stared at my new boots.

"I wore mine out," I told her, but that didn't keep me from getting a sneer.

Once she'd finished her beans, she tossed her plate my way and grabbed a blanket I'd found in among that missionary mess. Then she retired into the scrub, and the first night that's where she slept.

Since I didn't know exactly where we were, it was hard to say where we were going. I couldn't be sure which town we might be on a course to come to next, but I did promise the girl I'd deliver her into the hands of civilized people.

"Church folk and them," I told her, which she seemed undelighted about.

I would come to learn she'd been treated poorly by those missionaries. Not just her, but all the children. It seems that bunch had a strap they used on the kids when they got wild or mouthy. Sometimes, she made me understand, they brought it out for nothing at all.

I promised her I'd find a better batch. "And if I can't," I told the girl, "you can just keep along with me."

That, of course, earned me pretty much the sneer my boots had raised.

The first week, she'd hardly walk on the trail but stayed in the grass and the scrub. I warned her she might come on a rattler before she had the chance to see it and offered to put her on my Comanche pony, but she shook her head and kept on walking. She'd eat what I fed her and then threw her plate at me, wrap herself in her blanket and lay down most anywhere. Otherwise, I hardly saw her because she stayed behind me all day.

So it wasn't like I had company, more like I was being
haunted. Even from thirty yards off, I could feel her staring my way.

I talked to Gunther about her, naturally. He had to
be suspicious too because she displayed no interest at all
in what him or the pony might be doing. Most children
would either be loving them up or making mischief with
them, but she couldn't spare the two of them much of
a look. She scowled at me when she wasn't peering out
across the landscape, and she didn't do that in a general
way like she was taking in the splendor of the plains but
more like she was worried trouble might be catching up.

Truth be told, I stayed worried too because there was
a regular world of hurt and bother to stumble across out
there. What you wanted to see when you looked around
was just the odd jackrabbit and maybe a cowbird or a
falcon overhead, and that's what we had for eight or ten
days while I kept us west by north a little. But then a rider
closed on us. He was moving at a trot, and we saw him
coming for a while.

I was relieved he wasn't a Comanche but just some rag-
gedy soldier from one of the forts around. They were out
there in force working to tame the savages and drive them
off their land.

I didn't know anything much about the army, had a
cousin who'd served in the CSA only as long as it took to
desert, so I could see this man had stripes on his sleeves,
but I couldn't tell what they meant.

Once he'd finally got up to us, he just said, "Water."

As we weren't oversupplied with the stuff ourselves, I

gave him a missionary canteen that was already about half
empty. He drank most of it and poured the rest over his
head.

He pointed at my pony. "Comanch?"

I nodded and told him my story about finding her loose
on the plains.

"Going have to claim her," he said and then aired some
brand of army mumbo jumbo about the powers he had to
ride up on folks and take whatever he pleased.

I decided not to agree or disagree to any of it but just
stood there wondering what might become of me if I shot
down a corporal or sergeant or (possibly even) a colonel.
That was the sort of stuff that came into your head when
you were strapped to a Colt Navy. Back home on the
farm, I'd never much thought that killing was an option
because you'd go to jail and find yourself strung up after a
while.

Out on the plains the calculations were all of a different type, and the going urge was to make damn sure you
gave it before you got it. Savages around were just living
up to the name, but it was different with the white folks.
We were chiefly from back east where we'd lived by decent
limits and had been raised to think that homicide was a
long way from alright.

It paid, out on the frontier, to overhaul and rejigger
your standards because you wanted the buzzards to peck
the other guy.

While I didn't much care if that soldier commandeered
my painted pony, since the thing was too skittish and
bony to be of much use, I decided if he laid claim to any-

thing else, I might just draw my pistol and shoot him.

"Who's that?" he asked of the orphan in the scrub.

I sifted through what I could tell him and opted for, "My sister."

"What are y'all doing way out here?"

"Got family." I pointed west-ish.

He named some town.

"Yeah. Near there," I said.

"Raiding parties around."

I nodded like I was already well aware.

Then he pulled out his pistol, and I feared that maybe I'd miscalculated and should have already given him two from my Colt. But he swung that gun of his around and pointed it at his horse. He was about to let fly when the girl started shrieking.

He held off to say, "He's broke down, sugar."

She let up long enough to draw a fresh breath and scream some more.

"Leave it for me," I told him. "Got to do some explaining first."

He didn't much care how his horse got dead. He shrugged and then started shifting his tack and his saddle to the pony. His bay was sweaty and chewed up, more than a little bloody from spurring, but that horse seemed hardly in the kind of shape that only a bullet would fix.

The girl came up while I was watching that soldier go. She made one of her noises at me before laying a hand to the snout of his mount in a tender sort of way.

Once she'd laced her fingers together to show me what she needed, I gave her a leg up, and she settled in on that bay, perched on nothing but his wet back. She grabbed his mane and laid over on him while both me and Gunther watched her. Then she made one of her noises, and that horse made one of his. That girl never walked through the scrub again.

In the weeks that followed, I can't really say I came to understand her, though I did learn more about her. I found out her name was Belle once she'd spelled it out in the dirt.

She'd lost interest by then and couldn't even muster a snort.

I was supposed to be going to California. We'd missed the big gold rush by a few years, but our thinking (me and Frank and Calvin) had been we'd work around the edges and find the veins left for us after all those other boys had gotten rich and quit. We didn't, of course, know anything about gold mining, though Calvin had found a ruby once while he was messing in a creek. We'd all figured we'd learn what we needed when we had to learn it. The draw, in truth, was mostly leaving behind the drudgery of where we were.

Aside from a dead sister, I also had two brothers. They were twins, and they were ten years older than me. Momma and Daddy had hoped to have more kids before I came along, but one was born dead and two or three others never got that far, so I have to imagine they'd kind of quit on it before I came along.

It was hard back home having brothers as old as Lester and Leonidas because by the time I was six or seven, they were in their meanest years. Since there were two of them, they could take turns picking at me and thereby guarantee I never got a break. That's how it felt anyway, and with every year older, they gave me more of their chores so they'd be free to cat around.

They chased girls, most particularly the ones who had no stomach for them, and that was a healthy assortment because (the talk was) my brothers had suffered in the womb. People said they'd gotten mashed together due to how my mother was a dainty thing, and that explained why they'd popped out smushed and homely. Lester was lopsided, and Leonidas had an uncommonly skinny head, so you could certainly make a case that they'd been cramped to poor effect.

That doesn't account, though, for how mischievous and wild those two boys were. Daddy never could do anything with them. He'd wear them out, but none of it ever curbed my brothers. Folks hated to see them coming. They never let up and tormented me to no end.

So Frank could get locked in his cellar and make his peace with staying home, and Calvin wasn't adventurous. He'd only agreed to come along because he'd once talked to a man who'd gone on at length about the mountains way out west. For my part, I'd had enough of my brothers and was sick of doing all their work, and I knew how mad my Daddy would be once he'd seen I'd taken Gunther, so there were plenty of reasons for me to keep going after I set out.

The gold, then, was part of it, but the distance between me and home was part of it too. And my trip already was both better and worse than I'd planned for and expected.

One dead Comanche on the good side but dead missionaries as well, and now I had a sneery child to try to stick
some place.

We did probably four weeks of westing, before we came
to an actual town. It had a store and a dance hall, a church
and a stable, a few houses near a graveyard and some
ranches here and there. It was called Little Cabot but only
on one sign, and somebody had knocked that over. A man
who claimed to be a deputy marshal told us the town was
full of people who'd moved over from Big Cabot. It was
situated on the Cimarron and got swept away in a flood.

A lady in a carriage came clattering up and stopped
alongside us.

"Just y'all?" she asked.

"Yes, ma'am."

"Going where?"

"Kind of working that out."

Then she aired her own style of toot and told us both,
"Come on." She smacked her horse and off she went, never looked back once.

There wasn't far to go. She led us up past the church,
which had been built on a scrubby hump of ground and
was a ramshackle piece of work. If you knocked the cross
off, it could have passed for an ambitious shed. Her house
was behind it. She called it the parsonage even though it
came off as barely a shack.

"Mr. McBride has passed," she informed us but failed to
enlarge or elaborate, so I only learned in time that she was
the widow of Mr. McBride who'd been the local preacher.
He came off, the way she told it, as something like Epis-

copalian, but the frontier version that did without the silk and crockery.

"Heart," she said and then paused to pray, so I stood by and let her.

"You need a scrub," she told Belle and then sized me up with a look. I got a lump of soap and pointed to a pond behind the church. More of a mudhole with some dead bushes in it.

For Belle, she dragged a copper tub into the yard, even heated water for it. I wasn't sure Belle would stand for all that, but she didn't come off as especially sneery and put out.

That pond was smelly and there was a toad on the bank about the size of my hat. I spied what I took for a trio of snapping turtles, so I didn't plunge in and failed to get clean enough to satisfy Mrs. McBride. She made some disappointed racket once I'd come back to the yard and ended up scouring grimy patches I'd missed with her finger and some spit.

"Can't I get in the tub now that she's done?" I asked.

She told me that would be sinful. That was the trouble for me with Christian folk. You never knew where they'd draw a line.

Mrs. McBride gave Belle a proper cotton dress to wear, and Belle only tooted a little. The woman had me kill a chicken, and she cooked it up with turnips and some kind of stringy green. Her grace at the table was brief and to the point. She gave thanks for our safe passage and then directed a few remarks at her preacher husband looking down.

"This is awful kind of you," I told her. Belle even made an appreciative noise.

"You're free to speak, young miss," the widow said, so I started in explaining as best I could about Belle and everything.

She let me carry on at length with whatever I felt I needed to say, and once I'd gone from Virginia pretty much to Little Cabot, I finally quit talking and left her a gap to ask me, "And all of this for gold?"

What could I do but look ashamed and nod.

"There's a place," she tapped the table, "for you right here." She was talking just to Belle.

"How would that work?" I asked her since Belle wouldn't.

"I'd raise her as my own, with the sweet Lord to bless and guide us."

I feared a sneer and toot were coming, so I headed them off with a kick.

I let Belle have the rope bed, and I stretched out on the floor beside it. That house was just one big room, and the widow was snoring under a pile of quilts across the way.

"There are worse spots," I told Belle. "Plenty to eat, and she doesn't seem that bad."

Belle made a symphony of noises, which I took at first to mean she was maybe half conflicted, so I made a bid to nudge her.

"You can keep the horse," I said.

She squeaked at me one time out of her nose and decided to leave it at that.

Since I wasn't in any hurry to get back on the trail, I was

willing to stay for a day or three and help the widow Mrs.
McBride with repairs around the parsonage and inside the
sanctuary. That gave Belle some time to get a sense of what
life in Little Cabot might be like. Clearly, it was the better
place for her since I couldn't say how far I'd go or what
kind of scoundrels I'd run up on, and California was over
the mountains yet and a heck of a stretch away.

Gunther, I could tell, was delighted to pass some time
in the parsonage side yard where he ate rye grass and
stomped at chickens, rolled around in the dirt. That bay
was improved by the slack time as well. He'd only needed
to get himself out from under that soldier's saddle, and
Belle babied him and tended to him, made her noises in
his ears.

For my part, I leveled up three pews and put a cross
brace on the pulpit. I replaced some busted window glass,
spread oakum on the roof, and whitewashed about an acre
of siding clapboards. And that was only in the church. The
parsonage needed a fair bit of new flooring, and the pastor's widow had me level up and rehang both her doors.
Luckily, I'd learned how to be handy doing all my brothers' work and more than a little of my daddy's as well. So
I just needed three days for everything and finished up on
Saturday evening. I would have left the following morning, but the widow insisted I be in church.

That was fine with me because she'd promised Sunday
dinner and I was facing a stretch of almost exclusively
beans. I couldn't tell exactly what Belle was thinking by
then, but I'd gotten the sense she was sort of settling into
the place. I had even seen her laughing once or twice out

in the yard. She never kept it up for long but could have passed, at least briefly, for an ordinary child.

The pastor's widow was a gracious hostess and only something of a scold, which is fairly high praise for a Christian lady. So come Monday, I was persuaded I'd likely be heading west alone.

Belle had left early and taken her horse, was nowhere around by the time I had Gunther packed up and ready to go.

"We all cope how we can," was the explanation the pastor's widow offered while I was thanking the woman and politely taking my leave.

"I'll make a proper young lady out of her," she said. "Might even get her talking."

"Tell her bye from me," is how I left it, but I could have told her myself because Belle was waiting out where the Little Cabot sign was laying in the dirt.

I felt touched that she was seeing me off, and I made a couple of sentimental remarks and raised a salute that she snorted about. Then she tooted and sneered and followed along behind me on her bay. For an hour. Then two. Then all afternoon. She tossed her empty plate my way at supper.

I can't say I much minded being haunted out there again.

3

He was mostly down to bones when we found him. Scraps of cloth. A little leather. Everything else had been plundered already. I knew him by his teeth.

I wouldn't have gone over if Belle hadn't insisted. We'd seen the buzzards circling, but I'd reached my limit with dead stuff. Since we'd left Little Cabot, we'd come across a wealth of carcasses. Buffalo. Coyote. A couple horses. A half dozen elk and antelope and deer, along with some kind of prairie cat I'd never seen before. Most had been skinned and butchered with all the best meat taken for salting. Delaware Indians chiefly is what I'd come to find out.

I'd assumed those buzzards were marking more of the same and didn't want to break off to see it. So me and

Belle disagreed in the style we often did. I'd say, "Nope." She'd toot at me and back and forth we'd go. This time it lasted until she left the trail while I kept moving.

We'd come to be independent that way. She'd do what she pleased, and I'd go how I wanted. But then she whistled, so I knew it was something I had to see after all.

From what was left, you couldn't say for certain how he'd met his end, but he'd sure been pilfered by whoever had killed him or found him first. No boots. No guns. No cartridge pouch. No tent canvas. No canteen. No hat. No knife. No Comanche pony. Just bones in a pile mixed with bits of strapping and tattered scraps of trouser.

I couldn't quite believe the brand of racket Belle then chose to make.

"No ma'am," I told her. "I'm not burying him."

But then she tooted it all again, and I knew there'd be no shifting her from it. She'd stand there tooting until doomsday, so I pulled out my shovel and started on a hole. It didn't need to be a big one since he'd come entirely to pieces and could be tumbled in any old way. Belle did me the courtesy of staying handy to get sniped at while I dug.

That was our customary practice. She'd make me do a thing and then hang around so I could resent her while I did it.

Belle insisted on some sort of benediction, so I committed that sergeant or corporal or colonel into the care of God and reminded her he would have shot her horse if I'd held my peace and let him. She didn't find any of it satisfying and made me pray all over again.

Back home, there was a man we all knew who couldn't

be relied upon. His word was no good. His promises empty. Though he'd surprise you every once in a while, he stayed shiftless most of the time. Belle was exactly the opposite. She somehow always knew what was needed and made damn sure it got done and done the proper way. I barked against her plenty at first, found her willful and peculiar, but I got educated and came around in time.

That isn't to say she wasn't willful and thoroughly peculiar, but there was far more to it than I'd noticed early on. She had intuition and instincts and knew how to act upon them. More like premonitions, if I'm honest, and I learned to hear her out. Whatever direction she wanted to take, whatever velocity she preferred, that's exactly what we did and how we did it.

But at first I did resist her. She was some child tooting at me and in no shape to truly explain herself. So we'd be going along, and she'd make a noise or three and then work her fingers in a bid to tell me something. I could almost never decipher what and so usually kept on going. But then one day she went so frantic that it would have been wrong not to stop.

"What's up with you?" I asked her.

She held up a finger to let me know I'd see the cause in time. I would have snorted back if that finger hadn't saved me a week before when she'd kept me from sitting right on top of a moccasin. The weird thing was she was almost certainly too far away to see it. I was half down a creek bank while she was over messing with her horse.

So I had that episode in my head when she held up that finger again. Me being me, I immediately looked around

for a rattler, and by the time I got back to her, she had that
finger to her lips. They were so close, I could hear them by
then, and I caught a flash of scarlet through the scrub. I
couldn't tell much except that they weren't white.

They were crossing before us, heading due south with
the bulk of them on horseback. They didn't look painted
up enough to qualify as Comanches, but the sad truth out
there was about any of them would leave you dead and
scalped. The army was making such ruthless war on most
of the tribes all over that you couldn't be white and blame-
less anymore.

We held our ground and held our breath. She tooted in
her horse's ears while I rubbed Gunther in his spot in a bid
to keep him quiet. Once it was all beginning to feel like
we'd lucked out and gone unnoticed, a dog broke off from
the bunch of them and came through the scrub our way.
I say dog, but they never quite looked like anything you'd
see on a farm, were usually more in the way of a creature
you'd get if a coyote loved up a goat.

This one had fur all over his back in clumps he'd yet to
shed. He was spotted in an unflattering way, and his eyes
were two different colors. He came right up to us, showing his teeth. I had my gun out ready to shoot him, but I
couldn't think that would solve awful much. We looked
done for either way.

Belle, though, had a racket for that dog, and he sat right
down to hear it. Those two appeared, for all the world, to
come to an understanding. Once she'd finished with him,
he just got up and left.

We'd had a witch back home, the sort who'd cast spells

using sprigs of hair. She'd cure sickness by burying bloody rags in the woods and would blow grate ash on you if you were down with heartache. She was a warty, old thing and the only witchy type I'd ever seen, so it wasn't like I was tempted to lump the likes of Belle in with her just because the girl had made a dog sit down.

It did seem possible to me, though, that Belle was out of proper balance and so could see and hear maybe better than most because she couldn't talk.

I tried to draw Belle out on the matter, was ready to hear whatever she'd tell me, and that was even before she went out in the scrub and brought a rabbit back.

We'd been making do with beans and had gotten low on jerky, so I'd gone off with my rifle to kill something we could cook. I can't say I was ever much of a shot. My daddy did most of our hunting while I was in charge of tilling our field and growing what we could. Most anybody could kill a Comanche from probably about four feet, but that didn't translate to me taking aim and bringing down our supper. So I went out with just my rifle and came back with just it too.

Belle, of course, had a noise for that, which I took for ridicule, but it was probably more on the order of *let me go do something for you* because she struck out through the scrub and stayed gone for a little bit. The rabbit she came back with was half again as big as her, and it looked like she'd somehow slipped up on it and bashed it with a rock.

She skinned and gutted it with my knife and skewered it on a limb for cooking, and I was too pleased to be eating meat to press her much after that.

My thinking on Belle evolved after the dog and then the rabbit, and I came to suspect, because she was a mute and born unsanctified, that she'd been blessed by the good Lord with something like the skills of Daniel Boone. That fit into my view of a world where Jesus kept things level. He was the giving sun, but He was the sickle too.

It helped that she went back to doing just the stuff she'd done before, making sneery noises my way and telling secrets to her horse. I kept her from having to go in the scrub and brain another rabbit by catching two actual fish, big fellows, each as long as my arm. One of them I caught anyway. The other I shot once he'd failed to cooperate. I think they were some kind of frontier carp. They had plenty of good meat on them, and we hauled those fish and ate them until the smell finally put us off.

Usually, I'd walk ahead with Gunther behind me, and Belle would trail along in back of him. On her good days, she would chirp and snort, and her tooting would go musical. On her bad days, she'd make no noise much and come off seeming glum. There wasn't anything like a world of difference between one and the other. Her mood would only ever rise or fall a few degrees.

For my part, I wasn't steady at all. The farther I got from Virginia, the madder I was at Frank and Calvin for making me strike out alone. Sure, we'd talked about the gold we'd pan and the foolish ways we'd spend it, but primarily we'd been anxious to get out in the wide world alone. The more I trudged, the surer I grew I'd never go back home, which would have felt better if I'd had Frank and Calvin with me. I tended to shift from mad to sad with a stop or

three at hungry, and it got to where Gunther would say
with a look he'd heard all he could hear.

So we were a pair, me and her, but as I think back, our
moods did seem to coordinate. She'd be up and tooting
when I was sulky, and I'd often be half jolly those days she
fell off. It was teamwork, after a fashion, and that went
for our foodstuff too. Once we'd run out of fish and jerky,
that girl somehow bagged a woodchuck. It was greasier
than rabbit but better than just beans.

We traveled for a stretch without seeing anybody, no
savages but no civilized people too. For a considerable
while, we were still in Oklahoma but veered over into
Kansas territory for a bit. I think we did anyway. I'd failed
to make any strides much with my plotting and was a bad
one for getting the stars wrong night to night. I could only
be sure we were keeping west and so would presently run
into an ocean.

I'd put from my mind the idea that I'd end up stinking
rich and serve as a going temptation for all sorts of fancy
women. I'd had dreams of settling in with one in a fine
house out in Frisco, but that was before I'd passed untold
weeks walking across the plains with a girl who tooted at
me and a mule biting my neck. Those two had the effect
of overhauling my plans and expectations. Instead of
Frisco and fancy women, I wanted a steak and a tomato,
a mattress no matter how lumpy, and a private outhouse
where I could pass an entire afternoon.

So that's where I was—plateaued some distance south of
where I'd started—by the time we caught up with a wagon
train on the Kansas side of things. It was a batch of Ger-

mans with minders they'd hired to keep them safe on the
trail, and those guys were as close to gunfighters as anyone
I'd seen. They all wore double-pistol rigs and never strayed
far from their rifles, could have one shot of whiskey and
quit, and worked in shifts both night and day.

Only a couple of the Germans could speak any English,
and one of them was the special assistant to the big boss
and chief who had a mole in the middle of his forehead
I couldn't help but fix on. That thing had more hair on it
than some people and was a couple of different colors, so
when I was talking to him, that mole was about all I could
see.

I was just trying to find out if it would be alright for
me and Belle to ride with them for maybe a week or two.
The boss wasn't so sure because his group was some special
strain of believers. I got the sense they were on the order
of evangelical Masons but worse. They all dressed alike in
these smock-looking things, and the women had to look
at the ground whenever a man came near. The men made
signs at each other with their fingers and often muttered
some form of prayer. That's what it sounded like to me
anyway. We'd had a pack of Irish neighbors who'd done
the Catholic version of that sort of thing but usually loud-
er and about half drunk.

I'll admit I was in it primarily for the cowboys with
the double rigs since I was worn down with worry and
vigilance and in dire need of relief. Those fellows seemed
capable of protecting us, and I was ready to unclench, so
I agreed to everything the boss required. It wasn't a lot. I
had to join in with the other men when they prayed, and

Belle needed to get in the habit of looking at the ground. When I explained that to her, I got a snort I'd never heard before.

In the end, they kind of left us alone, so I didn't do awfully much praying, and Belle looked wherever she wanted most of the time. Those Germans stuck together, and the cowboys did as well, so it was me and Belle like it had been before but just traveling in among them. We'd get a kind word every now and then, and that bunch proved content to feed us. More beans. Some cabbage. Salted bread. And often one of those double riggers would bag a pronghorn or an elk. The Germans would cut them in funny pieces and cook up bits I'd have thrown away.

I got to thinking we'd stick with that crew as far west as they'd let us because it was nice not having to worry about much of anything day to day. I usually walked with Gunther between a couple of wagons while Belle rode on her bay wherever she pleased, ordinarily off in the scrub and behind us all.

It went like that for a stretch before, late one morning, Belle had one of her episodes, by which I mean she knew what was coming before it came. I wouldn't call it an ambush exactly. We just ran into some Pawnees, and things got livelier than they had much call to be.

I only knew they were Indians, had no idea what flavor until one of those double-rigged cowboys shouted out, "Pawnee war party!" and those fellows all pulled their guns, so I pulled mine.

The difference between them and me was that they all started firing. There was a stumpy hedgerow up ahead, and

I could see people just beyond it, but I couldn't begin to tell which people and what their business might be. So I held my gun to have it handy, but I didn't shoot at anybody. Those cowboys weren't so particular, and they were shooting double-handed. A few of those Germans had grabbed rifles, and they were shooting too.

Not much came back. A couple of arrows and what sounded like a musket ball, and then there was the usual yipping and yelping as those Indians took off. Those cowboys eased up past the bushes and the spindly trees. They came back through with an old Pawnee woman who looked half shot to pieces and an Indian boy who seemed unharmed. He was carrying a dog, about twenty pounds worth of the usual specimen that appeared to be molting and starving both at once.

Those cowboys threw the woman down. You could tell she wouldn't pull through. Then a couple of them started shoving the boy, and one of them grabbed his dog by the scruff. It tried to bite him but couldn't quite make that work, so that dog wriggled free and ran straight over to Belle. It sat behind her.

The cowboy with the greasy chaps and the mustache that nearly reached his shoulders smacked that Indian boy around for a while and then kicked him some as well. Once he'd pulled a pistol, a German woman came over to object, and she planted herself between that fellow and the Pawnee boy until the big boss with the wart sent some men her way to pick her up and shift her clear.

The fever, though, was off by then, and the fellow with the mustache said, "Hell." I guess he thought shooting

that Pawnee boy might feel too much like murder, and
instead they tied him by a length of rope to a singletree.

The Pawnee woman had long since expired. She looked
to be shot in three or four places, and once she was clearly
dead on the ground, those Germans got religious. They
gathered around her and prayed.

When nobody made a move to bury her, I was the one
who got the toot and didn't buck against it or fight it
because I knew that wouldn't help. I just pulled out my
shovel and stayed behind with Belle and that ugly dog
while the rest of those folks pressed on ahead up the trail. I
didn't get even one offer of help from any of the Germans,
and the cowboys each made sure I knew they took me for
a fool.

"What do you think they'll do with the Indian boy?" I
asked Belle while I was covering up his auntie or mother
or whoever.

She had a noise for that. A couple of them actually,
which added up to a heck of a lot more than *Can't be sure,
don't know.*

We didn't catch up with the rest of them until a little
past suppertime, and they appeared to have decided feed-
ing that Pawnee boy was more trouble than it was worth.
They'd tied him to a wagon wheel with both of his hands
behind him, and he looked to have made part of that
afternoon's walk on his face. They might have missed the
chance to kill him quick, but they seemed fully prepared
to help him along with dying over time.

And I don't mean just the cowboys. It was that bunch
of God-fearing Germans too. I saw a few of them kick

the boy, and several spat on him and cursed him. One of them caught me looking and explained in his English he had friends who'd gotten dead. By which he meant from Indians generally I think, but since he couldn't catch up with that lot, this Pawnee boy would do.

His dog visited him a little but mostly hung by Belle, and one of the cowboys started quizzing me on Belle's dog rearing technique. It turned out he was from Indiana and had only been cowboying for a while. Before that, he'd done pretty much what I'd been up to. Farming. Keeping chickens and cows. He'd been a big hunter too and told me he wished he'd had Belle's sort of touch with his hounds.

"Couldn't do nothing with them. Tried. But look at her," he said, and me and him together watched Belle have a chat with that Pawnee's dog. Her kind of chat with toots and snorts while the dog stomped its front feet and whimpered.

"What are y'all going to do with him?" I asked about that Pawnee boy.

That fellow plainly couldn't be bothered to care.

"Can't turn him loose now," he finally said. "He'd be sure to come back hot."

I know it might sound like I'm leaving stuff out, just skipping over the back and forth that me and Belle got up to. But that wasn't a chat we needed to have because I could well guess what she wanted and knew exactly what my part in it would be. It wasn't like things could go on with that Pawnee boy dying some each day. I might not have understood the weird stuff Belle could do, and I wasn't altogether settled on how I felt about it, but I was sure we weren't about to let things go on like they were. Hell, our mule and our horse were more decent between them than that entire pack of people.

There was no caper much to it. I just cut him loose one night. He'd been with us a day or two shy of a couple of weeks by then and had gotten, I'd calculated, as knocked around as he could stand. He might have been Pawnee and used to living rough and raw, but nobody could hope to endure that kind of treatment for long.

He didn't try to run but followed me away from the wagons and climbed up, at Belle's invitation, right behind her on her bay. There were a couple of cowboys making circuits, watching the livestock and the Germans, and one of them was the Indiana guy with the hounds he couldn't train.

When he saw who we were and where we were pointed, he touched his brim with his finger and went off another way.

We put some miles between us and that wagon train, dipped well south before turning west again. The idea was to run along in the general direction of that bunch but far enough off to stay out of their sight. That way, if we got into trouble, we'd still have cowboys and Germans handy.

Of course, that all depended on me being aware, from day to day, of where we were and which way we were going. I put on a show of having a better grip on that stuff than I did.

I thought, at first, Pawnee boy could probably help with star reading. Since he was a savage, I figured he had all grades of frontier skills. But I soon discovered he wasn't that kind of Indian at all. He didn't like walking, wasn't big on gathering firewood, and usually couldn't be bothered to help unpack Gunther evenings when we'd set up camp.

He wasn't exactly lazy but was in the general vicinity of it, and he complained quite a lot in Pawnee, which we couldn't understand. You could tell by his whining tone what he was sort of up to, and every now and then he'd throw in his only word of English. It didn't help much because it was *howdy*. He had a knack, though, for saying it like the effort made him tired.

So my chief company was a girl who couldn't talk, an all but worthless Indian, a willful mule, and a dog with probably a muskrat in the woodpile. That soldier's horse was about the only regular thing we had. I half believed even Comanches wouldn't find us worth their while.

I'll confess for a stretch there I kind of lost sight of what exactly I was up to beyond shifting stuff and people across the landscape every day. We made steady westerly progress, but I couldn't decide where I hoped we were headed. I knew any town would be a problem for that Pawnee boy and his dog, while Belle still needed to catch on with some upstanding family, though I feared most of them would be like the reverend's widow in Little Cabot—religious to some degree or another and not much of a fit for the girl.

I still dreamed sometimes of California and the chance to do some panning, but I didn't get around to it in any regular way. I had the charge of those two while I was still little more than a boy myself. I soon kind of missed being out on the open plains with just a mule for company.

We didn't see anybody at all for something like two

weeks, and I was half thinking we ought to veer a bit
north and get a read on those Germans when, instead, we
happened across some squaws who were traveling on foot.
They weren't Pawnee but spoke some language our boy
could pretty well understand, and him and those women
had quite the lively, involved conversation. They'd pause
here and there to look at me and Belle and then chew the
fat some more. Belle didn't seem too bothered, but I felt
powerfully uneasy.

That bunch reached some sort of agreement, our Pawnee boy and all those women, and they soon made it
known that me and Belle were to come along with them.
Three or four of the ladies had stuff to say to us, and our
Pawnee boy chimed in as well, and by the way they waved
their arms around, we could kind of tell what was up.

So they all went on ahead, and we came along behind.
As best I could tell, we were on a course that was south of
west a little and so was putting some distance between us
and those Germans with their cowboys. Consequently, I
kept reminding Belle that it would soon be us out there
alone.

She didn't seem much concerned. The child was only
maybe ten, so I can't really say why I was taking my cues
from her except she'd kept me from sitting on a snake and
could talk to dogs a little. That put her a couple of notches
above my mule.

Those squaws didn't do much talking as we moved
along, and once our Pawnee started complaining—we
were maybe an hour in—one of those ladies caught him
by the arm and smacked him once on the head. It turned

out all he'd needed was a touch of motherly abuse because
he quieted down and stayed that way for the rest of the
afternoon.

We hadn't gotten anywhere to speak of by the time we
lost the sun, and when we stopped, nobody built a fire or
tried to organize a campsite. It was the Indian way, apparently, to just sit on the ground and do nothing instead.
Those ladies shared jerky with us. It must have been prairie
dog or something like it because it was rank in a verminy
way and too hard for human teeth to chew. My human
teeth anyway. Those squaws appeared equipped to grind it
up.

Then they stretched out on the ground right down in
the dirt, each with a ratty piece of deer hide for cover.
When Pawnee boy's dog wouldn't bed down with him, he
launched into some complaining, but then one of those
Indian ladies groaned, and that was enough to scare him
dumb. Me and Belle slept in the dirt as well with that
Pawnee boy's dog between us. Come daylight, I woke up
to find a squaw with a finger in one of my ears.

What she said, once I'd opened my eyes, had more ver-
biage to it than I could handle.

"I'm up," I told her and moved to sit, but I discovered I
couldn't do much at all until she'd pulled her finger free. It
was a hell of a technique, and I wished I'd known about it
when I was fighting off my brothers back home.

They all didn't exactly wait for us but went off like the
day before and left us to hustle up and follow them or not.

By midday I was telling Belle that we'd get some actual place that evening or me and her would break off and

head out on our own the following day.

Belle gave the impression of being agreeable.

It didn't come to that, though, not just then anyway because about midafternoon we reached a place I wouldn't quite call a village, but it seemed a little too built up for a camp. There were teepees of the sort I'd only ever come across in drawings and huts built out of skins and limbs and spackled up with stream mud. I saw pigs in a pen made out of saplings and horses hobbled across the way. There was some kind of guinea fowl running loose all over the place and scores of dogs even homelier than our Pawnee boy's specimen.

The Indian men didn't pay much attention to us, not to me and Belle anyway, but a slew collected around our Pawnee boy. A few of them appeared to quiz him, but most of them seemed to be picking at him. They pulled his hair and poked him, relieved him of his pair of leather briefs and then had some fun examining the Pawnee manhood they'd exposed.

Pawnee boy took it all well enough. He didn't look to me to be complaining but gave back a couple of doses of guff and got a rise out of that bunch. He appeared to be a different creature in among his type and we were the ones being uneasy and doing nothing. Then a man with feathers all stuck in his hair came over and said a lot to us in whatever language that pack of people used.

I didn't know what to tell him back beyond making a try with, "Howdy."

He said a couple of more things, and then me and him both looked on as Belle raised a hand to show him her palm and grunted at him in a complicated way.

He eyed her in what looked like wonderment to me.

Then me and Belle got busy watching a woman walking in our direction. She was quite a sight out there in the middle of all that Indian clutter and mess. If she had a tribe, hers was probably out Donegal way. She was a redhead with freckles, and she was wearing the remnants of a gingham shirt along with a wrap for her southern bits that looked to be pony hide. She wasn't much cleaner than the rest of them. That was a dusty, dirty bunch. But she moved our way like a lady who'd crossed a parlor before.

She took her time reaching us, had to show proper courtesy to the Indian men she met along the way. She'd dip her head and say a word, which would earn her (it looked) their blessing to proceed. Then she'd press on until the next guy came along. So we had plenty of time to wonder who she was.

When the woman finally reached us, she gave us the full once over, and I mean me and Belle and Gunther and Belle's bay and the Pawnee boy's homely dog. Once she'd finished, all she said to us was, "Well."

It was a relief to hear English from her, something other than *howdy*, and I took the chance that she had more words by asking the woman, "Who are these folks?"

I had a glance at the general population standing out among the tents and lodges and the various livestock pens between us and a far marshy patch where some kind of stream appeared to run.

"Cheyenne," is what she told me. "Who are these folks?" She was looking at us. She did sound a little Irish but mixed with something else. Maybe, I figured, a touch of New York too.

"Kind of a long story."

"Isn't it always."

Belle tooted.

"What is it, princess?" she asked.

So I had to lay out the state of things and how the two of us had come to be together.

"How'd you get here?" I asked her. Grabbed up somewhere, I guessed.

I'd read about girls snatched from outposts and wagon trains and then hauled off to live in teepees while their menfriends all searched for them. After a while, they'd get to where they were like Indians themselves. This one sure looked the part, especially from her gingham shirt tail down.

"Wasn't like that," she said.

"They're not going to keep us here, are they?"

"Comanches, sure. Apaches sometimes. But this lot?" She shook her head. "You in a rush?"

I told her we weren't and allowed I was just wondering.

"Here he comes," she said and pointed out a man across the way.

At first glance, he passed for an Indian. He was strapping with long dark hair, and he had on hides and feathers and strings of beads and was wearing the sort of knife on his hip you could almost surely bone a missionary with.

He struck me as a fellow on the mean side of things until he looked over our way and saw the lady we were with. That lit him up, and he was doing something pretty close

to smiling by the time he arrived where we were. That's
when I noticed she was doing about the same. He grabbed
her up in his arms when he reached her and kissed her so
comprehensively that Belle had time to toot and snort and
warble a little as well.

When they pulled apart, we got from them both a
proper introduction. She was Orla, from Dingle originally,
and he was Arturo from Guadalajara, but he told us the
Cheyennes all called him *Mahpo*. He tried to explain why.
It was something about water, but me and Belle weren't
equipped to figure it out.

Orla invited us to stay with them in their tent and
wouldn't hear of us heading off or pitching the tent that
Gunther was hauling. Arturo allowed the Mexican part
of him would be insulted, and those two together seemed
keen to show us wholesale hospitality.

When Belle didn't buck, I thanked them and allowed
we'd stay overnight in their teepee and probably take off
come morning.

"For where?" Arturo wanted to know.

I told him we were due to meet up with some Germans
on the trail.

"North of here," I said, though I do believe I might have
pointed east.

"I knew a German," Orla informed us and then took
Arturo's hand. "Didn't I?"

He nodded and said, "*We* knew a German." Then they
kissed again.

We stood there with things weird and awkward for a
moment before me and Belle and all our critters followed

those two out towards the stream where we watered Gunther and Belle's bay, that Pawnee's dog a little as well.

I got a sense that evening that Orla and Arturo were chiefly happy to talk to white folks. They both appeared to know enough Cheyenne to get by, but they seemed more stuck on each other than their Indian friends were built to appreciate.

Those Cheyennes weren't a romantic people. Most anybody could see that. They certainly did what nature demanded. The place was crawling with Cheyenne kids, but there was nothing resembling tenderness that passed between the men and women. Life was hard, and they all had jobs to do. It could have been they snuggled up later, but nothing in the way of romance was out on public display.

Orla and Arturo, on the other hand, were plainly hungry for each other to a pitch that made me uncomfortable because I'd been raised to think it wrong. My folks did more of the Cheyenne thing, so their children truly seemed like miracles because we only saw them chafe and carp and quarrel all the time. Arturo, however, was gallant. In their teepee, he would have pulled out Orla's chair if they'd had one, but instead he held her fingers lightly and helped lower her to the floor.

That was the first teepee I'd ever been in. Even still, I felt sure it wasn't normal because they had an oil lamp and a chamber pot, what looked like an end table with a picture leaning against it, a handsomely painted portrait of a man in a frilly shirt.

Orla caught me looking at it. "Joseph," she said. "My

dear brother." She laid the back of one hand to her lips while Arturo stroked her hair. It was like they were up on stage, and me and Belle had bought tickets to see them.

"You probably want to hear our story," was the next thing Orla said.

I can't say that was high on my list of stuff I probably wanted to do, but when you're a victim of hospitality, you have to go with whatever's offered.

"We," she started, "Fritz and I, had only just arrived in Oneida."

I didn't know where that was and couldn't remember a Fritz, but Orla struck me as the kind of roundabout talker who'd clear everything up in a while.

Orla and Fritz had taken a room at the only lodging house in Oneida, and Orla started in painting for us a picture of the place. The garish decor. The clumsy folks who ran it. The failure of the staff to take much care with their spittoons.

I was settling in for an epic, since that seemed to be Orla's way, when we heard a shout from outside, a burst of Indian yelling, which was quickly followed by our Pawnee boy showing up inside the tent. He came shooting on in, found his feet, and said a lot of stuff right at me.

He seemed something past agitated, more on the order of drunk.

Arturo and Orla heard him out. "Upset about his dog," Arturo told us.

Arturo suspected he'd been into the liquor they made out of some kind of root. He gave it a name that hardly sounded like a word and let me know it was awfully powerful stuff.

"How old is he anyway?"

Arturo asked our Pawnee boy how many years he'd
passed on his earth. The number he told me, I could hardly believe. That boy was twenty-three.

Orla stepped in to explain how those Indians didn't get
the right food or proper care, which some of them could
manage while others came up short.

Then Pawnee boy launched hot into a run of talk that
Arturo endured before turning to me.

"You're going to have to fight him," is what he said.

I felt like I could take a twenty-three-year-old who
could easily pass for fourteen, but I'd been on the trail so
long, walking day after day, that I wasn't sure I could spare
the energy.

"For what?" is what I asked.

"He says," Arturo told me, "you stole the spirit of his
dog. Not you exactly, but her." We had a look at Belle.
"But he won't fight a girl."

"It's not to the death or something, is it?"

Arturo doubted it was but couldn't say for sure since he
was still Mexican primarily, so he put the question to our
Pawnee boy who said something lively back.

Arturo told me, "Might be today."

5

Since I was all about the balance of life back then, I had to think me fighting that Pawnee was offsetting my Comanche, the Maker's way of evening my stuff up. I tried to stay calm about it all, or at the very least polite. So I didn't sneer at Belle for having swiped the spirit of that Pawnee's dog while all I did was cook beans for them both and endure that boy's complaints.

Because that Pawnee boy was a runt and sloshed on fermented root, I can't say I was terribly worried about taking him on as an opponent. I might have been only sixteen, but I had twin older brothers, so I'd been obliged to fight with them and their friends in order to stay alive. I did, though, worry a little about the Cheyenne braves around. I feared some of them might want to fight me once I'd

put that Pawnee down. That was how drunk white men
carried on. First just two of them would be brawling, and
then everybody watching would get charged up and bust
whatever came to hand.

"How about," I asked Orla and Arturo, "I go out and
apologize to him in front of anybody he wants."

They were amused, those two, and cautioned against
that brand of sensible response.

"Drunk Pawnee," Orla said and shook her head like it
was hopeless.

"I just hope I don't kill him." I told Orla and Arturo
about my Comanche and explained my thinking on debts
against righteousness.

"You grab," Arturo told me. He showed me where and
how, but Arturo was a strapping man with brawn in all the
right places while I was just some lanky guy who'd lately
been walking in front of a mule.

"Ain't fair," I said. "Wasn't me messing with the spirit of
his dog."

I'd been thinking it all along and couldn't help but blurt
it out. There's a natural limit to how considerate any boy
can be, and I was still underdeveloped where it came to
polite restraint. So I said what I said and glared at Belle.
She tooted and shot me a sneery look while Orla took the
break in chat as a chance to return to Oneida. She said
she'd been on an excursion with her brand-new husband,
Fritz.

"He worked for my father," she told us. "I may have
even thought I loved him, but..." Orla turned moistly Arturo's way, and the two of them found each other's hands.

"We were on our way to meet a man up in Denver City. He was with the railroad. I never got that far."

Arturo lifted Orla's hand to kiss and/or swab her knuckles. He said something in French, I believe it was, that turned out to be a poem.

"It was called The Belvedere," was the next thing Orla told us, and then she passed nearly a quarter hour cataloging the gimcracks and decor in the lodging house where they'd stayed. Flocked wallpaper and velvet settees. Gas lamps. Crystal. Hand-buffed silver.

"That first night when we gathered for libations, well…" Now it was Orla's turn to kiss and swab. Those two were quite the pair.

It seems Arturo swept into the parlor of that lodging house in Oneida. He'd stopped off on his way to somewhere too. When Orla saw him and he saw her, that kind of cemented it for them.

"The heart, you know," Arturo said and tapped his chest with a shiny, swabbed finger. I think he was trying to tell me the damn thing would do what it pleased.

I got it. I'd been in love before or something kind of like after seeing a girl by a hayrick once with the morning light on her just so. It was painful to be taken with her and not even know her name or where she lived or if she had a slew of beaus already.

She turned out to be older than she'd looked and sort of regular up close, but I was still interested enough to have a run at her, and she proved keen to find out about my brothers. That took more of the shine away, so I didn't stay smitten for long. But I believe I had some sense of what

Arturo must have felt.

Orla too, to hear it from her. She snapped her fingers. "Like that," she said.

"You didn't kill Fritz, did you?" Throughout my life, I've only had so much patience for a yarn.

Arturo looked to Orla who told me, "I'm sure he's past it now."

They snuck off two nights later. That was all it took for him and her. They got together to talk things through when Fritz went out to buy a hat and Orla stayed behind at the lodging house having raised a complaint about vapors.

"I hoped he'd come," she said of Arturo who'd been so bold as to knock on her door.

"You take, yes?" Arturo said my way, and I understood him to mean if you can't steel yourself to grab what you want, you may very well never get it.

Those two were sufficiently feverish about each other to sneak off from Oneida even though Arturo had just one horse and a wife expecting him back home while Orla left in only her gingham blouse and the skirt she'd been wearing. That's passion for you. It'll mess everything right up.

Orla said she'd written a letter for Fritz, but he decided she'd been obliged to write it under duress, especially after a boy at the stables remembered his wife taking off with a Mexican.

"He gave chase," was how Orla chose to put it, and it sounded like Orla and Arturo had done what we'd done for a bit. They came across a wagon train and stuck with it for a while before getting freshly uneasy about Fritz and striking out on their own again. Same clothes. Same horse. They still had between them next to nothing. To hear Orla tell it, they met up with a Cheyenne hunting party just when some of the shine was dulling off of what they'd gone and done.

"*Mi amor*," Arturo little more than whispered.

"Dearest *Mahpo*." That was followed by another bout of swabbing.

Then Arturo aired a couplet about how the heart might flag.

Those Cheyenne Indians took them in, even gave them a teepee and some deer hide clothes, and failed to scalp them and kill them, which had to count for something.

"Three months ago now," Orla said and didn't come off exactly thrilled.

Arturo reminded her they'd soon be traveling to Mexico City and leaving grubby teepee living behind. Orla, however, looked like a woman who'd been reminded of that a few times before. But then they took turns kissing knuckles and appeared to be a pair of people devoted to each other like actors on a stage.

"They bite," was the next thing Arturo said, and he was saying it to me. "So fingers, yes?" He made two fists. Then he tapped his nose as a warning as well.

"How do we know when it's over?" I asked him.

He yielded to Orla. "You will."

Then they escorted me and Belle outside. I figured I'd meet that Pawnee boy maybe over by the pig lot and we'd go at it until he was satisfied that he'd avenged his honor, or whatever a Pawnee needed to feel to know he'd fought enough. But that wasn't at all how things would play out because the Cheyennes had gathered in what made do as their village square. Even the chief was there, or at least an old guy in a fedora and a bead and bone vest who was sitting in an actual chair that appeared to have been upholstered once.

The men were passing around a skin full of something that they'd squirt in their mouths and hand on. More fermented root, I had to think. Every time it went near that Pawnee boy, he took a double dose.

I wasn't much worried about him but was more concerned about all the drunk spectators who just knew me as some white guy who'd shown up at their place. I seemed dispensable even to me. I wasn't sure where I was and couldn't conceive of who'd come looking if I got buried in an anthill or strapped to a tree or pummeled for a while with a rock. I'd read all about what Indians did and was wishing at that moment I hadn't.

Belle tooting at me didn't much help, but it did attract that Pawnee boy's dog. He came running up from the creek bed where he'd compounded his homeliness by getting muddy right up to his ears. He passed that Pawnee boy without a glance and ran straight to Belle. He failed to jump on her and muddy her up but instead gave her hand a loving lick.

Those folks all saw it and knew what it meant. The spirit of that Pawnee boy's dog had, in fact, been stolen. Probably by the girl, but I'd have to answer for it.

So over we went, and Arturo advised me to strip down to my drawers. I was reluctant to but only because I felt white enough already and knew what a pale spectacle I'd make in just my underpants. But Arturo insisted, so off my clothes came, and I immediately got jeered at by a whole bunch of Cheyenne who were red by birth and filthy by practice and possibly had never seen a human as unpigmented as me.

Then Arturo and Orla started translating the rules of the contest as they were hearing them from the old man in the chair. He made it clear that we'd be wrestling and he'd tell us all when he was satisfied we'd gone at each other enough.

The old chief gave a shout, and Pawnee boy came at me about as fiercely as any scrawny drunk Indian could. He was furious. I couldn't begin to miss that. I'd seen him angry out on the trail, but it never lasted long before he lapsed into pouting. You can't have no gumption to speak of and stay mad for very long.

It could be he was just an angry drunk. I'd seen plenty of those in my day and was related by blood to a few of them, so I figured it would only last until he got groggy and dozed off, and I was in a good spot to help him along with that.

I wanted to punch him, but since we were wrestling, I grabbed him and wrenched him around instead, and damned if he didn't find some flesh to bite up on my shoulder. I yelped. Aside from my sister, I'd never been bitten by a human, and certainly not one with such malicious intent. He drew blood, and the crowd whooped and hooted. All I thought about in that moment was keeping the boy away from my nose.

He weighed almost nothing, was just five feet of empty skin, so I hoisted him up and flung him, which the crowd approved of as well. I was happy to hear it since I didn't much want them cheering that Pawnee alone. Being drunk, he was slow to get up, which gave me the chance to inspect the plughole he'd made up by my neck.

I got hot just looking and called out to Arturo, "Can I kick him?"

He told me, sadly, "No."

"Well come on then," I said to that Pawnee boy and waited for him to reach his feet.

Me flinging him had made him cautious, so he circled and went strategic. As strategic anyway as a sloshed Pawnee boy could get, which wasn't enough to anticipate that I might do some charging, so I barreled at him and bulled him over, knocked him clean off his feet. Then I dodged away before he could locate another piece of me to gnaw.

Life would have been a heck of a lot easier for me if I could have just punched him once, but I could see Arturo watching me and shaking his head, so instead I stayed where I was and lobbed at the boy a couple of insults. I told him his dog probably just didn't like him and then added he was so stinking shiftless that I didn't like him too. Of course, he couldn't understand me, but the mere act of taunting the boy bucked me up and almost made me forget the turn my life had taken. I was standing in front of a pack of Cheyennes, most of them lit on fermented root, wearing nothing but my underpants, which weren't as clean as I would have preferred.

I would have washed them more, but they were all I

had left because my other pair had gone to pieces. Many a
day, I walked for miles and miles with nothing on beneath
my trousers, so I was lucky to have been wearing that pair
when I had to shuck my pants. That was the sort of stuff I
was thinking about to keep myself from kicking the fellow
and just stand there waiting for him to pick himself up
and come at me again.

   He did get back to his feet in a little while, but he headed straight for a quencher. The hide full of root juice was
still making the rounds, and that Pawnee boy grabbed it
and helped himself to a considerable squirt. Then the chief
made a declaration, and Arturo said, "You too."

   He pointed me to the root juice. Ordinarily I would
have resisted. We had drinkers in my family on my daddy's
side, and my mother had seen enough of that sort to raise
us to take only water. Both of my brothers broke loose
once they got married, and they were bad ones anymore
for loading up and shoving around their wives. So I'd kind
of seen enough of drink, but you work up a thirst wrestling Pawnees, and I got the feeling the chief wasn't actually making a suggestion. I could tell by how he pointed and
the look he shot my way.

   So I went over and grabbed the skin, squeezed a stream
of the stuff in my mouth, and then did the work of trying
to swallow it because that liquor was god awful. I didn't
get a chance to smell it but could imagine from the taste
that it probably stank of mold and dank and rot with a
hint of blistering alcohol. It burned and repulsed at the
same time. I desperately wanted it out of my mouth but
could see all of them looking at me. That meant it would

be leaving in only one direction.

So I swallowed and focused myself on working to keep it where I'd put it, and I felt like I'd done a heroic thing when all that came up was a burp. But I could see they wouldn't be satisfied until I'd had another mouthful. Isn't that the way with drunks all over. They always want you worse than them.

This time, they wouldn't even let me squirt it but made me stand in front of a brave who was well decorated with feathers and bones and black and yellow gashes of paint. He had dark smut all around his eyes and looked like a raccoon, a mouthy raccoon because that man said quite a lot in my direction. Orla tried to translate for me, but that brave wouldn't have it and barked out a thing or three until Arturo had stepped in. The fellow didn't seem to think a woman was up to telling what he'd said.

It wasn't much really. "You step back," Arturo told me, "until he says."

So I backed away from him and stopped when he told me something complicated. Then that man squirted in a showy fashion and failed to even hit my face. The stream of root mash sailed past my left ear, which got a rise from the chief and the general Cheyenne population. It was enough to make that brave mad, so he bore down and hit my mouth. Not at first but only after he'd sprayed the stuff all over my face.

It tasted like something you'd find between your toes or grease a wagon axle with. Plus it was hot going down and, shortly, coming back up as well.

That meant he had to spray liquor all over again because one of their Cheyenne rules, apparently, was that you kept their root mash in. So I swallowed some more and clamped down my teeth. This dose I managed to hold onto and earned the kind of cheer from the Cheyennes around that even I could tell they didn't mean.

Then I had to fight some more. That Pawnee boy reminded me of it by hitting me with a fencepost or something like it that he'd scrounged around and grabbed.

I raised a protest naturally, shouted, "Hey!" a couple of times, and most of the Cheyennes gathered round laughed and shouted it right back while I was dodging that Pawnee boy and coming to understand that Cheyenne root mash was some powerful stuff. I'd never had a drink of whiskey. I was just a boy, and a boy in a family with so many men down the line who'd been ruined by liquor that my mother made sure none ever got kept in the house.

That meant it got kept in the barn instead, and I'd been cautioned by my brothers not to touch it. They weren't worried I'd turn to drink but simply didn't want any less for them. So I was a virgin where it came to alcohol. At the time, I let that account for why I got to be so wobbly, but I've had plenty of bonded liquor since then and so lay the blame these days on the power of that Cheyenne mash. The stuff worked like poison. It got in you and took hold.

That Pawnee boy was accustomed to it. He was twenty-three and looked fourteen probably because he never let the liquor skin get past him without helping himself to a squirt or three. He was sloshed but could still function while I could barely stay on my feet.

I know now it wasn't a fencepost he had but just a stick
of wood, and not even a particularly hefty one, hardly
more than a piece of kindling, but I was so gone on root
liquor that everything around me looked monstrous and
odd. The people all came across like freaks, especially Belle
and Orla who appeared to be howling at me and floating
off the ground. The chief in his chair looked four or five
times bigger than he was, and I thought for a moment
there Gunther had wandered over to say a thing, or to ask
me anyway, "What are you up to?" in a weary, muleish
way.

All the while, that Pawnee boy was abusing me up and
down, hitting me with sticks and stuff and knocking me
over when he could, and it seems that I kept climbing
back up to invite a little more.

That's the limit of what I remember. I think he sat on
me for a while, but I can't be sure of that. I might have
only dreamed it once I was sleeping off the root mash in
Orla and Arturo's tent. Orla was swabbing me with a rag
when I finally came around.

"What happened?" I asked her. It took me three tries.

"Balance is restored," was all she said. She swabbed me
some more, and then Arturo showed up to look me up
and down and groan.

I think I was three days recovering. That's how I recall
it anyway, but it was hard to tell because I was stretched
out on top of a buffalo hide and couldn't see much but
the hole up where the teepee didn't quite close, so I wasn't
fully aware of what was going on.

I do remember hearing Orla kind of explaining the

world to Belle. Orla's world chiefly that had grown small
for her and had come to be constricting.

"Honey," I heard her say, "some people don't count as
much as they should."

I came to understand she meant Mexicans, maybe Indians a little too, but Orla's specific problem seemed to be
with folks who wouldn't tolerate a woman like her with a
man like Arturo just because she was from one bunch and
he was from another.

"Funny, isn't it?" is what she said to Belle, but I could
tell even in my condition that wasn't what she meant at
all. It was why they'd ended up where they were—in a
tent with a pack of Cheyenne—because decent people in
civilized places had decided they didn't belong.

Belle yielded up to Orla some toots I'd never heard
before. Then she growled, or that's what I thought anyway
until I'd shifted enough to get a look at that Pawnee boy's
dog beside her. I immediately had to worry (because I'm
a fretful sort) that Belle would get Orla and Arturo ban-
ished by the Cheyennes too. They might have been ready
to shear your scalp and read their fortune in your entrails,
but they weren't about to tolerate a dog inside their tents.
Not for themselves and probably not for hangers on as
well.

So first I was worried about the dog and then about that
Pawnee boy because I wasn't just foggy but sore all over
and didn't much hope I'd meet the chance to wrestle him
again.

Along about then, Orla shouted for Arturo who came in
through the door hole with, of all people, that Pawnee boy

right behind him. Naturally, I announced I wasn't in fit shape to fight.

The Pawnee boy had a speech to deliver. I could tell he'd planned and rehearsed it by the way he'd get half through a part and then start all over again. He talked only to the teepee wall, and Arturo and Orla took turns translating, though they were only good for those bits of the thing that veered closest to Cheyenne.

The gist of it was he'd vanquished me but was prepared to be gracious about it because he could see that Belle—he pointed at her—got on better than him with his dog.

I couldn't make out any of it on my own. Back then, all Indian sounded to me like so much racket. Lots of clicking and chuffing and elaborate hand waving, which I couldn't begin to piece together. It was like standing under an oak back home and listening to a squirrel.

But here was Orla and Arturo passing along, when they could do it, the sense of what that Pawnee boy was saying. Essentially, it turned out he sought my forgiveness for having beat me with a stick.

"Alright, yeah," I tried to tell him, but that came out like yodeling. The root liquor still had ahold of my tongue, which they all seemed to understand, so that Pawnee boy made plans to come back and get forgiven later while Orla swabbed me some more with her rag. I don't think I required it, but that seemed to be the only nursing she could do.

I came around once I got some deer meat in me and a couple bowls of Cheyenne soup that the tribal medicine man brought over once word had gotten out I was poorly.

He was old, and wrinkled and dusty and wore a cougar skull on his head. He shook over me some kind of gourd that I found out was full of teeth because he dumped some out and made a show of shaking them in his hand. He blew dingy white powder on me as well and sprinkled me with something oily, and that was all before he handed over a hollowed rock full of soup.

Orla anyway insisted it was soup, but it wasn't hot, was as thin as water, and was full of what looked like tent floor sweepings.

"Am I supposed to drink this?" I went to the trouble to ask her even though I already knew I was and was trying to put it off for a bit.

Then the medicine man spoke, and Arturo said that the fellow would have to examine me further if I didn't take his soup. All he had was a knife and what looked like the business end of a busted arrow, and I sure didn't want to get doctored on with either one of those, so I drank down that soup full of twigs and mess, and I do believe it did what it was engineered to do. I suddenly found the strength to jump up and run outside so I could empty myself from both ends at once.

That proved to be all I needed, and I became so close to spry that the medicine man called in an audience to witness my condition as a way of further demonstrating how powerful he was. They all examined what I'd discharged and engaged in a discussion about it, which was just when the Pawnee boy showed back up to get properly forgiven.

I didn't know the right words, and since neither Arturo or Orla was close beside me and handy, I just threw my arms around that boy and gave him a kiss on the cheek.

The medicine man saw me do it along with that pack of Cheyenne who'd come to examine my poop. They got together and talked through what to make of the show I'd put on before they decided the Pawnee boy and me were brothers for life, which served to make his dog my dog as well and so settled the entire business.

The Pawnee boy insisted we celebrate with root mash, and those Cheyenne were more than willing. They were fonder of drink than even my uncles who I used to find in the corn crib or under our porch after one of their nights. I was allowed, because I was shaky still, to let Pawnee boy have my dose, and him and the tribe went on a tear that lasted a couple of days.

Once I'd recovered and gotten back to something like normal, I realized I was itchy and bored with Cheyenne village living. It wasn't moving me closer to California, and those folks (for my taste) were a touch too lively and loud. They didn't hoot and yip quite as much as Comanches, just judging by the one I'd killed, but those Cheyennes barked and warbled plenty, and it probably didn't help that I never quite knew what they were going on about.

In the back of my mind, I lived in fear I'd have to wrestle again and go through the ordeal of mash and soup and general evacuation before forgiving whoever I needed to forgive.

So it could be I was too anxious and fragile to have much use for Cheyenne life. All I know is that, as the days went by, I started organizing to leave. That first meant taking charge of Gunther who'd gotten accustomed to going nowhere and doing it with no load at all on his back. Consequently, he didn't want to see me coming and raised a muley stink. Him and Belle's bay had done nothing for days but eat scrub and roll in dirt, and Gunther let me know he'd be content to keep that up for a while.

I had no idea who'd be coming with me, which is to say I'd kind of lost my read on Belle. She'd done nothing approaching peculiar through our whole stretch with the Cheyennes. I'd talked her up to Orla and Arturo, and they'd passed a bit of that along to a few choice Indians they knew, but Belle hadn't done a thing to back me up. The girl mostly sat in the teepee. She did it some with Pawnee boy's dog, but she was just as happy on her own perched cross-legged on a blanket.

When I told her I was leaving, it wouldn't have surprised me if she'd snorted and tooted to let me know she'd given up on traveling the plains. That's not how it went, though, because Belle didn't snort or toot at all but instead pointed to direct me Orla and Arturo's way. They were outside the teepee just then holding court.

Regularly, not daily but often, they'd go out front and be romantic. They'd embrace and nuzzle, kiss a little, just make shows of tenderness that always attracted an audience of otherwise unoccupied Cheyennes who appeared to find Orla and Arturo confounding and exotic.

For his part, Arturo seemed deeply invested in the healing power of love and the balm of poetry, which tended to set aside the fact he was living in a teepee among Cheyenne because him and Orla had made a scandal. She was married, and he was Mexican. Folks hadn't even gone so far as to care that he was married too.

I remember sitting in the teepee with Belle one time while Orla and Arturo were out front being cozy. They had their usual audience of Cheyenne gawkers who'd come to watch them embrace.

"What are they even doing?" I remember saying.

That raised a toot from Belle, and it wasn't at all the brief, sneery type of toot I usually raised but was something on the order of contemplative (I'll call it) and more than a little sympathetic like maybe some part of Belle was prepared to half believe in romance as well.

So I thought she might stay on with Orla and Arturo since they were all saps together and could go on in a bunch believing true love ever got anything done. I didn't buy it. I had a mule with a big personality and a destination down the road, so I was all right paring back to just the way I'd started. That didn't mean I wasn't ill about it, but I told most of that to Gunther while I gathered my goods and loaded him up. The Cheyenne came around with gifts. Jerky. Herbs. Some kind of stinky salve along with beads and feathers and bones. Finally the chief called me before him and uncorked a wealth of palaver before presenting me with a huge knife in a deerskin sheath that was cut in with decorations and beaded everywhere beads could fit. It had an antler handle and an edge you could have shaved with.

I was touched and told them, "*Hahoo*," every way I could think to say it. It was Cheyenne for *thank you* according to Orla, and it was a word I'd met occasion to come out with quite a lot. They were decent people for savages, if a little too loud and dirtier than I would have liked.

Back at the creek, I found Belle on her bay. She had Gunther's reins and was waiting for me. That Pawnee boy's dog was down in the mud watching everything she did. Belle didn't toot or sneer but just gave me charge of Gunther and then led us through that village out the way that we'd come in.

I told her I hadn't known the chance to say goodbye to Arturo and Orla, and I wondered what the Pawnee boy would think about her leaving with his dog.

She couldn't be bothered to respond until we'd reached a wide spot up the trail where folks were waiting for us. Arturo, Orla, and Pawnee boy as well. I figured it for a sendoff until I saw the stuff they'd brought. They had one pony between them, a pitiful looking scrawny thing, that Orla and Arturo had loaded down with a couple of carpet bags and the painting of Orla's brother. There was a blanket bundle too with Pawnee boy's meager goods inside it.

I wanted to lay out for them all my faults and trailbuster deficiencies, but they'd seen me around enough to watch me operate or fail to, so I guessed they knew what they were in for, which I boiled down to merely, "Welp."

That homely dog went charging up the trail. Orla told us something in Irish. Belle loosed one of her sneery toots, and off across the plains we went.

Methuselah's Toenails

1

We only had the one tent, and Orla was wearing exactly the wrong shoes, but she claimed the Cheyenne moccasins she'd brought along didn't do it for her either.

"Oh, *Papi*," she'd say to Arturo on those occasions she'd reached her limit, and Arturo would beg us to ease up and stop for a bit. He didn't need to beg us because we were on no particular schedule, but Arturo never missed a chance to indulge his dramatic streak. He had a knack for pleading, would ball up his hand and hold it in front of his face and then come out with a sonnet or something like it.

Orla tried to ride their pony once or twice, but it was too broken down for that. If that colonel or corporal were still around, he would have certainly shot it.

At least Orla and Arturo had packed some food. That Pawnee boy had brought a skin half full of mash and hardly anything else. He told Orla who told us that he was hoping to dry out because he said root mash worked a brand of dark magic on him. When I offered to pour out what he'd brought, he pulled his knife and objected. Then his dog growled at him, and he howled back like a wolf under the moon. I decided I liked that Pawnee boy better when he was full of complaints and lazy.

We ran across a bad omen our third day out. Belle had one of her premonitions and loosed a toot to stop us cold. She didn't seem clear on why or how long, which means it wasn't much like the fits and visions she'd had before. This one was cloudy for her. I was equipped to tell that much.

So we stopped and we sat and we waited until Belle felt our way was clear. Then we pressed on and hadn't gone but a little ways before we came across a ball of rattle-snakes.

I'd met up with a couple of those before back home in the mountains. We were thick with rattlers, and they'd get all balled up in the spring. It was a mating thing, and usually we'd have at them with our shotgun so as to keep them from biting us later when we were tromping through the woods.

That would have been spring back home, but there we were in summer, and those snakes looked more in the way of fighting than doing anything else.

We just needed to go around them, but that proved a difficulty because they were musky and tangled and rat-tling and striking, just eating each other up. How could

you not believe we'd come upon a significant thing? And
Belle's premonition had slowed us just enough to see it. I
couldn't help but stand there wondering what it meant.

Being Irish, Orla hadn't grown up around snakes and
so didn't know enough to be alarmed. She was fascinated
instead, especially once I told her that snakes all over only
balled up to mate and that I'd never even heard of them
getting in a tangle to kill each other. That's plainly what
these snakes were doing, and there were two dozen of
them at least. Big diamondbacks, each with a head the size
of a silver dollar.

Pawnee boy couldn't leave them alone. Indians love to
mess with snakes. I'd seen a bunch of Cheyennes fooling
around with a rattler the way regular people might pick at
a cat. They were taking turns snatching it up and putting
parts of it in their mouths, and then they'd let it strike
at them and dodge away without, somehow, getting bit.
They smashed it with a rock once they were done since
they weren't completely daffy and didn't want to flop
down one night on top of a snake that they'd provoked.

That Pawnee boy found a stout stick and started poking
and stirring up trouble. Those snakes were too preoccu-
pied with each other at first to pay him any notice, but he
turned out to be more diligent with his snake antagonizing
than I'd known him to be about virtually anything else.
So soon enough he got a snake or three to strike his way
and try to bite him, which raised more howling from that
Pawnee boy in a show (I do believe) of delight.

The rest of us just wanted to skirt around and get on up
the trail. Me and Orla and Arturo anyway. Belle, for her

part, seemed distracted. I think she might have been troubled and a little confused over how her premonition had
hit her and what exactly it meant. That's what I figured at
the time based on how I'd seen her be when she was spar-
ing us from other trouble while we crossed the plains. This
snake thing wasn't so cut and dried and seemed to weigh
on her a bit. So she stayed perched on her bay in tootless
and squinty contemplation.

Soon enough, that Pawnee boy had managed through
uncommon diligence to redirect all that reptile animosity
his way, and damned if those snakes didn't get untangled
and squirm loose on the ground. Sure they were peeved
with him mostly, but they were prepared to bite us too.
Gunther and that Cheyenne pony as well, who both
bucked and scrabbled backwards. I didn't know what to
do but pull out my Colt and fire a couple of rounds, but
it's no easy thing to hit a snake, especially one stretched
out on the ground.

We saw the wisdom of retreating back the way we'd
come, all of us but that Pawnee boy who stayed in among
the reptiles hooting and howling and poking and yet failing somehow to get bit.

Those snakes soon enough had the same reaction to
him the rest of us did, which is to say they wearied of him
and went off to their snaky business, which freed him up
to come our way all full of Pawnee talk about everything
we'd lately seen him do. Arturo knew better than to bother
to translate any of it for us but instead tolerated Pawnee
jabber and gave some Cheyenne jabber back.

Along about then, I noticed a change had come over

Belle. She'd shifted off of her cloudy expression to one that was noticeably clearer and had even managed to toot once before we heard a yip. It came from off towards a hump of ground. I'll say it was to the east, and there on the rise where we could see them were four horses and four riders. I wanted them to be white and civilized, but they came off as savage instead. They howled and yelled and charged our way. I had to think my gunshots had brought them.

While I was drawing my pistol and maybe enjoying my hair for the last chance I'd have, Orla helped herself to the rifle stowed in with the stuff on Gunther's back.

It had been my grandfather's gun. By rights, it belonged to my brothers, but I'd taken it when I was packing to leave and got off before they'd noticed. It was a Winchester Repeater, and I wasn't completely versed on how to even use it. I'd killed a squirrel with it once back home but I'd not even been shooting at him.

I kept waiting for Orla to ask me how exactly the thing worked, but she was too busy shifting that Cheyenne pony to where she could rest the barrel on him to steady her to aim. She plainly knew what she was up to, so I just stayed clear and watched. I couldn't help but notice Arturo was doing pretty much the same. He looked as surprised as I felt but, of course, more romantic about it.

Orla let those Indians keep on coming, and they were galloping at us four abreast, all of them howling and hooting. One of them fired a pistol our way, but the bullet sailed way overhead.

Orla licked her finger to wet the front sight and drew her bead in no particular hurry. When she fired, the one

with the pistol left his pony with a yelp. Then she shifted
and picked off another one, and the other two grew dis-
couraged. They decided to go off and menace other people
somewhere else.

Orla didn't wait for us to ask how she'd learned to shoot
like that.

"A gentleman taught me," she volunteered. "Before
Fritz."

That last bit hit Arturo hard. He'd been living with the
idea that Fritz was the only man his Orla had dallied with,
and yet here was some other fellow who'd schooled her in
shooting. He was stricken and devastated, which is sort of
the trouble with his type. It didn't matter that we were out
in the wild with both snake and Indian trouble. An affair
of the heart was a thing he couldn't ignore.

So he had to quiz Orla and drew her aside to take a de-
tailed history. That left me and Belle and that Pawnee boy
to go out and check on Orla's work. We found the second
one first. I couldn't tell what he was. The man was wearing
just leather britches and nothing else. Orla had hit him
square in the breastbone, so he was as dead as you could
get, but the first one was fifty yards further and still rolling
around in the dirt.

I was tempted to think him Comanche because he had
on some cowboy's vest with a fresh hole in the front and
a hole in the back where he'd been shot clean through. I
don't know how he was hanging on and can't imagine how
he was crawling, but there he went, and he still raised a
hoot or two as he moved across the ground.

The Pawnee boy said something to me and pointed in

an energetic way. For once, I knew exactly what he meant
but pretended like I didn't because I wasn't entirely sure
that I could shoot that Indian dead. He would have killed
us if he could have, that much I was aware of, so I had all I
needed to justify most anything I did.

But when I'd shot my Comanche, I'd not had occasion
to think about it at all. It was shoot him or get gutted, and
that kind of thing is clarifying, but this Indian crawling
across the ground felt to me like something else. I was,
after all, just a farmer's boy who'd wandered off from Virginia where most of the Indians we had did some kind of
sawmill work.

I'd made a bid to prepare myself for the rigors of frontier travel, but shooting a man because he'll die anyway
and you're doing him a mercy is something that might
seem Christian until you've got the gun in your hand.

So I was enduring instructions from that Pawnee boy,
hearing nothing at all from Belle, and trying to work out
how exactly I might feel after I'd done it, when that Pawnee boy got fed up with me and brained the guy with a
rock. He hit him twice. I haven't been able to forget the
sound of it yet.

I might have shot that Pawnee boy instead if he'd not
pointed out the pistol. That Indian had been trying to get
next to it in the dirt.

"Oh," is what I think I said.

I fetched that gun and had a look. It was a single-ac-
tion Smith and Wesson. A fellow I knew back home had
owned one, and he'd even let me shoot it a time or two.
This one had somebody's name scratched into the bottom

of the grip. W.T. Grimes. I pictured him as a pile of bones somewhere.

I waited for Belle to try to make me bury those two dead Indians, but either she'd come around on that sort of thing or had decided they didn't rate it. Either way, she failed to raise a toot or indulge in one of her sneery looks, so we left those Indians where they were and went back through the scrub.

Arturo and Orla were still discussing the man who'd taught Orla to shoot, and it didn't appear to much matter to Arturo that he'd perished in a fall.

"You're some kind of good," I told Orla.

That set off a spot of muttering from Arturo. I think he quoted a snatch of poetry.

"Want this?" I asked Orla and offered up the pistol we'd found.

That proved occasion for an arch glance Arturo's way before she reached out and took it. She swung the cylinder out and checked it. Orla knew what she was doing, and that only served to prod Arturo more.

Orla helped Belle up onto her bay and said as she did it, "How'd she know they were coming?"

"It's like the thing with the dogs," I told her. "Something going on in there."

The Pawnee boy made a remark. I figured he probably wanted a drink.

"Spirit girl," Orla told me. "Says he's seen one like her before."

"Where?" I asked him.

His sense of direction was about like mine. He pointed

at the sky.

Just as we were set to move, I asked Belle, "How are we looking?" I was hoping she'd do some gazing around in kind of a spirit girl way, but instead I got a sour look as she leaned down to toot at her horse.

So we were having a colorful time of it, and that was only day three. A ball of snakes, a batch of Indians, a fresh boyfriend in Orla's woodpile, and Arturo rivaling Gunther where it came to moody sulks. There was a half-eaten elk rotting in the only water hole we passed, and the spot we picked out to camp that night was overrun with spiders. Big, hairy things with white streaks on them that nobody minded but me.

We ate jerky and some kind of dried prairie apple. It didn't seem a good night for beans, and we didn't bother with the tent but just built a small fire and sat around it. Some of us stayed busy flicking spiders while others of us (Arturo mostly) spoke of plans and dreams.

He told us him and Orla had been taking a breather with the Cheyenne after falling in love in Oneida and then getting pursued to some dumpy little trading post where Arturo tangled with Orla's husband.

"Gave him a wound," is how he put it. There was a world of potential in that.

Arturo claimed to be disappointed that so few people around could stomach a Mexican man and an Irish woman in love.

"Are we not all the same?" Arturo asked and held high his balled up fist to do it.

It didn't seem worth the bother and subsequent quarrel

to tell him, "Not so much."

We didn't have Mexicans back home, but we did have a handful of Catholics, and nobody around was keen to let them stray out of their pack. The reasons were various and none too persuasive if you sat down and thought about them, but that hardly kept people from thinking what they thought. The difference was you couldn't really see a Catholic. They were devious that way. But you could glance at Arturo one time and know that he was Mexican even if he usually talked like a man from Texas.

Arturo said they next ran up on some fellow who treated his Orla like trash because she'd found the true path of her heart with a man from Guadalajara. Arturo announced he couldn't be held to account for the violence he might get up to if they met such a man again.

"Just give her a rifle," I told him, "and let her backup a hundred yards."

We took turns keeping watch that night because we were still uneasy since, out of four marauding Indians, Orla had shot only two. Aside from a couple of coyotes sniffing around, it was quiet most of the night until that Pawnee boy started singing a Pawnee song come dawn. There wasn't much music to it, just a mix of grunting and warbling, and I looked to find he was off in the scrub serenading himself while he peed.

"Are we not all the same?" I thought to myself. Back home on the farm, almost without fail, I'd whistle in the jakes.

Day four was better. No snakes. No Indians aside from the one we'd brought. And we came to a stream that was

still and deep enough to bathe in. Orla had even packed
two actual cakes of lavender soap, so we all got clean but
for Pawnee boy who seemed to prefer a generous coating
of dirt.

We damned up a piece of the stream we'd bathed in
and trapped a couple of flatheads that we cooked up with
greens the Pawnee boy gathered that tasted half all right.
And then instead of Comanches slipping up because we'd
built a fire, a very large white man riding a horse and
drawing a donkey behind him hooted a couple of times
from off and away to let us know he was riding in.

His name was Yasper, and he was a Swede two days out
of a place called Deakins. He was wearing fringed buckskin about everywhere he could possibly have it on, and
he'd grown a beard that reached his ribs but had cut his
head hair short with a knife. It was ragged and ratty looking, but he was proud of the job he'd done and so took off
his hat and bent over to show it to us.

He had his own food but agreed to some catfish once
we'd offered it twice, and he reciprocated with a jug of
something Arturo and Pawnee boy sampled. That Cheyenne root mash had cured me of ever wanting a drink
again.

He was full of talk, that Yasper, and told us all about the
town he'd left where they were gearing up to hang a boy
for stealing a string of ponies and killing one of the men
he took them from. It hadn't been murder outright. The
guy fell off his horse while chasing that boy and broke his
arm in three or four spots. He went septic, got amputated,
and then hung on a while but died.

"Killing's killing," Yasper told us before he laid his jug on his shoulder and drank.

He said he'd stayed in the hotel in Deakins for something like two months while he was resting up and recovering from a trip through the Dakotas.

"Kind of hate to do this," was the next thing Yasper said, and I was trying to work out what he meant when Belle tooted a couple of times.

Then Yasper's buddy came easing up out of the scrub and into the firelight. He had his pistol out and cocked and invited me to hand him mine.

He was named Hans. Yasper introduced him and explained in some detail that they'd set out to be miners but had instead become marauding Swedes.

"A lot of work, that mining," Yasper told us.

Hans threw in with, "Ya."

"We've got nothing worth taking," I assured them both.

"Could be," Yasper allowed.

Arturo moved to shield Orla in a gentlemanly way, but Hans with his pistol and Orla herself made motions to frustrate him from it while Yasper looked around to soak us in.

"Funny bunch," he said. "What's he?" he asked of Pawnee boy.

I told him, and Yasper grunted. It turned out he'd had a hard time with a Pawnee a while back.

"Was a cheat and a liar," Yasper told us. "Never could fix it," he said and then gave Hans a look you had to think meant *do with this one whatever you please.*

I got as far as, "Hold on," before Hans started shifting

around. Even the Pawnee boy knew what was up and ·
began singing a Pawnee song. There was little music to it,
just loads of grunting and regret.

When I heard the sound of a pistol shot, I expected to
see a hole in the boy but instead got quite a lot of Swedish
swearing from Hans as he jerked his bloody hand up high
and let his gun go flying. Orla's revolver was smoking from
the barrel. She'd managed to shove Arturo clear just in
time to get off a shot.

We were all stunned. Arturo was the one affected most
because he appeared to be both surprised and a little
aroused.

Orla trained her pistol on Yasper, so I stepped over and
took back my gun and helped myself to both of his as well
along with the knife he was wearing.

"Might ought to stuck to mining," I said.

Hans and Yasper both went with, "Ya."

Then there was talk from each in turn of where they'd
prefer to get shot. Not in the front or the back of the head
or just in the lungs somewhere but clean through the heart
and done from straight on if we could see our way to it. It
was a little jarring to have them yield so comprehensively
so quick.

Before we'd even begun to work things through among
us, I made a point of telling Yasper, "I'm going to need
that coat."

Honest-to-God fringed buckskin in the middle of Oklahoma. I couldn't pass it up even though that jacket was
more than twice the size I required. I figured I could find
a way to take it in and make something like a saddlebag

from the leavings.

Yasper explained he'd gotten that jacket off another guy, and so it only felt proper he should pass it to me.

Hans informed us he had a hole in his arm where Orla had pulled on him (he called it). He showed it to us and cleared the blood and suet so we could see straight through.

Orla sent Arturo after some worn out delicates she guessed Hans could have and use of. They turned out to be ladies underpants that Arturo tore into strips and then wrapped around Hans' shot arm and tied them off tight at the ends.

Hans was appreciative and said so. Yasper threw in with his gratitude as well.

"Y'all sure are friendly for marauders," I told them.

"Working for us 'til now," Yasper said. Then he paid strict attention to Belle for a bit before telling us all, "That one there's got the witchy eye."

"What makes you think that?" I asked him.

"My tongue itches," is what Yasper said. He then told us he'd learned to pay attention to his itchy tongue in Sweden and figured out it only happened around somebody with the eye.

"What's it mean, the eye?" That was Orla asking. She did it while also advising Hans to hold still by just wiggling her gun.

"Look at her," Yasper told us. Belle was handy, so we did. "She's seeing all we're seeing but everything else too. Aren't you?"

"She can't talk," I told him.

"Works that way a lot," he said. "*Fran avgrunde.*"

He only translated after a little while. He thought she'd come straight out of hell. I was skeptical. Belle didn't strike me as sneery enough for that.

Hans informed us he was hungry but there was no point in taking food if we were just going to shoot him through the heart like he'd requested. Yasper agreed it was probably time for that, so those two stood shoulder to shoulder and let us know they were ready to die.

"Hold on," I told them and called a meeting. Everybody got involved, even Pawnee boy and Gunther a little. He was a mule of many opinions and stuck his nose in where we were. Belle tooted at him and rubbed his snout and then shook her head our way.

"The girl from hell says no," Orla announced, and that was all it took.

We tied them up with bridle leather once Hans had eaten his fill, and they promised us they wouldn't go any- where. They were right where we'd left them come morn- ing.

We let them keep the donkey and most of the goods on his back but laid claim to their horses, which they both told us struck them as fair and proper.

"Deakins?" I asked as we were leaving and pointed pret- ty much the wrong way.

Yasper straightened me out by forty degrees and told us all, "Two days."

A ways up through the scrub we stopped so I could hold up and wave a pistol that we left for those boys on a rock so they might have a fighting chance.

They shouted (because they were both all right), "*Tack sjlav.*"

I don't even think it's a place anymore, wasn't terribly much of one back then. Deakins had one road down the middle and the sorts of buildings on either side that looked like they'd been thrown together straight from the timber mill. In the right season, a busted lantern would have taken it all away. And maybe one did because, from what I can tell, Deakins isn't anywhere anymore.

Back then, it was a rowdy spot. I'm guessing people had come in from all around for the hanging since that town was fairly bursting at the seams. We passed down the main road, took a measure of the place, and then kept on going for a mile or two until we found a spot to camp. The thinking was we'd work out what we needed by way of necessaries, and a couple of us would go back to pick them up.

Or I'd go anyway with probably Arturo and Orla because that Pawnee boy had made it known he was uneasy
in town. Any town, but especially Deakins where people
had gathered for blood, and Belle was about as cordial to
the place herself. It had a church and a shabby parsonage, which must have reminded her of Little Cabot. She
tooted to make me understand she wasn't prepared to be
do-gooder bait.

That was all fine. They could watch our stuff, and we
could feel sure it'd stay safe, overseen by an Indian and a
devil child. I told them both that, but they weren't much
amused—the Pawnee boy because he couldn't understand
me and Belle because she could.

Since we had to suspect those Swedish marauders would
likely head back to Deakins, we were determined to do
our business there as soon as we might and leave. So me
and Orla and Arturo got up early in the morning and set
straight out for town. They needed fresh tack for their
pony while I was after (God help me) more beans and
some kind of thread and needle I could work on my new
buckskin jacket with. There was salt pork to find as well,
along with a couple of blankets, and Orla required a pair
of walking shoes. Everything else was the sort of stuff we
could locate or do without.

So we split up once we hit greater Deakins, and I arrived at the dry-goods store just as the clerk was opening
for business.

He was excited. That store belonged to his Daddy, and
he told me they were making hay off the hanging crowd,

so much that he hated to see the boy strung up so soon.

"Just cause of business," he eventually said. "I hear that fellow ain't no count."

"He from around here?"

"Naw." He looked like he might spit. "Arkansas or somewhere. We don't much take to them."

"Right," I believe I told him and started quizzing him on thread.

I located Arturo off by the saloon where he'd gone hunting a bottle of sherry, but even I could tell Deakins was hardly a spot for that.

Arturo told me the Arkansas boy they'd soon be stringing up was in a stall down at the livery stable.

"No jail here. No law."

"Figures," is what I told him. "Did those Swedes have it right? Hanging for a man falling off his horse?"

Arturo had talked to the stable boy, and the best he'd been able to manage was, "Somebody got dead somehow," which was all they required in Deakins.

They'd tried the boy in the saloon. The preacher had stood in as the judge, and they'd found twelve nearly sober jurors to weigh all the particulars. He was condemned in maybe half an hour. That's what Arturo heard. And they would have hung him sooner, but the scaffold work got contentious because there were several bunches with different ideas on how you'd best ought to build such a thing.

They'd printed up handbills and sent them around to bring a crowd to Deakins and then had put off the hanging by three full days so they could soak the rubes. That's what they were up to when we were in town, which meant

we had to overpay for most everything. They didn't care
that we were just passing through and wouldn't even be
staying for the main attraction.

"Ain't life all in the timing," is what that store clerk told
me.

He wasn't far off. "Is today," I said.

We got out after a couple of hours. Orla ended up having to buy a pair of boots off a woman who she followed
down the muddy road and dickered with as they went
because she wasn't prepared to pay hanging prices in the
store. Then we had to load Gunther, who we'd brought
along for haulage, and got tangled up with a fellow who
came charging up all hot and red.

"Your damn donkey bit me," he told us all and showed
us a place on his neck.

"He's a mule," is what I said back, "and he don't bite."

"Then who did that?" He turned around to show us his
neck again.

Orla took over. "Friend," she said, "we don't know
where you've been."

"Right here getting bit by your damn donkey."

"What are you after?" she asked him.

He did the brand of math that required a man like him
to squint. "Three dollars," is what he came up with.

I gave him two bits instead. It was that or maybe ending
up in my own horse stall in Deakins for having defended
the honor of a mule.

That Pawnee boy was by himself in the place we'd
camped. When I asked him where Belle had gotten off
to, he pointed at nothing much and rattled off a bunch of

stuff in Pawnee.

Arturo and Orla between them couldn't manage to translate it all but did pick up that Belle had gotten excited and gone off. That Pawnee boy couldn't say excited why exactly and was disappointed Arturo hadn't brought a jug of something back. Arturo tried to acquaint him with execution pricing, but that stayed out of Pawnee boy's reach.

I went looking for Belle while Orla and them packed us up for travel. I didn't bother to shout because I couldn't imagine a toot would go too far. Instead, I found a hump of ground to stand on and had enough of a look around to spy Belle in among the scrub. I almost went back for the shovel, had a feeling I'd be seeing bones, but she was standing at the mouth of some animal den. A hollow in the bank where a stream used to run but was just dirt and rocks and scarred ground anymore.

There were limbs and mess clogging up that hole, and when I asked Belle what she was up to, she pointed at them.

That homely dog was out there with her, and when she pointed, it barked twice.

"Something in there?" I drew my Colt as I asked it.

She tooted in the affirmative.

"Can't we leave it?" I wasn't in a mood to tangle with a badger or some cat.

I got one of her other toots for that and the look I often earned.

"All right." I hunted up a stick I could poke at the scrub in that hollow and shift it with.

I didn't know what would come charging out and so got

cocked and ready, but I couldn't make Belle or that dog either one step back. They just stayed where they were while I cleared that hole to reveal some guy inside. He wasn't even dead and rotted but instead showed me both of his hands.

"I don't need shooting, mister," is what he told me.

"Come on out." I didn't holster my gun but also didn't point it right at him. He wasn't white and he wasn't black but was something in between. He looked about my age, or the age I'd looked when I left Virginia. I'd seen myself in a Deakins' window and had wondered who it was.

He was ragged and dirty and about the color of coffee the way my daddy would take it. His hands were bloody like maybe he'd dug that hole out just with them.

"What are you up to?" I asked him.

He appeared to rifle through his options. "Nothing," is what he finally chose.

That earned him the toot I often got.

"She doesn't think so," I said.

Once the dog barked, every quarter had been heard from.

"How'd she even find me?" the fellow wanted to know. If I hadn't seen her perform already, I would have been asking that very thing.

"She does that," is what I told him.

He studied Belle, gave a glance to the dog, turned my way finally for a look.

"Y'all from that town over there?"

"Naw. Passing through. You from Arkansas?"

He shook his head. "Louisiana. Wish I was back there.

Wish I'd never left."

"Horse thief? That you?"

"That's what they said, but I ain't never took nothing. Those men all tangled with each other. They just put the blame on me. I dug out of that barn and got away."

I didn't trust myself to judge him. I felt like I'd lost my bearings on that stuff along the way, but Belle was still clear in her mind and decisive. She heard the boy out and blessed what he'd said with a toot. Even the dog stopped barking.

"Got a name?"

He told me, "Ira," and then something Louisianan I couldn't begin to make out.

"They know you're gone?"

"Probably won't 'til supper."

"They seem keen to hang you."

"Yeah," he told me. "I was getting that too."

We all walked back to the campsite where all I needed to tell the rest of them was, "Belle says he's all right."

I veered us north off the main westerly route coming out of Deakins because it seemed certain they'd be sending riders searching for that boy. He told us he knew the man who'd died. He said he'd come off his horse full of whiskey and that ponies stole or otherwise didn't so much as figure in.

"I hired on with his bunch to drive cattle, but that didn't really pan out."

"Y'all fight or something?"

"Naw," he told me and said, "People get funny ideas about how things ought to be, especially once they're some way else entirely."

There was quite a lot of truth to that, and I would have said as much, but Belle stole my thunder with a toot.

We let him stick with us for a couple of days, figured it was temporary. He'd walk through the scrub off by himself and bed down out there as well just in case a posse happened through. On the fourth day, I believe it was, we finally saw somebody, and Belle let us know they were coming well before those fellows had spied us or we'd had any hint of them.

She snorted and tooted and raised her hands. Only Ira didn't know what that meant, but the rest of us had been around her enough to send him running for a spot to hide. We were out in the flats, so that wasn't so easy, but he went off to lay in some scrub while the rest of us poked along as four men rode up from the east. They weren't in an awful hurry and so only reached us after a while. Orla had the rifle out and my pistol was in my hand. That was just what you did out there, so those fellows took no offense.

"Boy kind of spoiled our hanging," was what they said, once the piffle and palaver all got sifted and boiled down.

They'd been paid to ride out looking by a pack of merchants in town who were hoping to keep the crowd standing by with the promise of an execution. So those four men were intending to round the boy up, but they weren't in any desperate hurry since those merchants were meaning to make that hanging last.

One of them described Ira for us but got all the details wrong. In his telling, the condemned man was as black as

coal tar and six and a half feet tall. *Strapping* was the word
he used and mean as Methuselah's toenails.

"Haven't seen him," I told those boys, and then Arturo
did the same.

"Don't kill him if you do, but you can kick him around
a little," one of those fellows advised us.

Another one volunteered that this boy they were after
had killed two men with a sword.

"Where'd he get one of those?" I asked him.

He laughed. "Where does his sort get anything?"

Two of those guys, as they were easing off, glared Pawnee boy's way and spit.

So we veered again, turned down to the south, and we
let Belle ride back on her bay to locate Ira and bring him
to us since she was the one with the knack for that kind of
thing.

They came up riding double.

"You chop up anybody?" I asked him.

"Is that what they're saying?"

"Some of them."

He did some snorting and shook his head.

"You know where we are?"

He nodded straightaway. "Oklahoma part of Texas."

"Which way you going?"

"Which way *you* going?" •

I pointed what I felt fairly sure was west.

"That'll do if I can."

I had a look around at Belle and Arturo, Orla and that
Pawnee boy, even briefly at the dog. It was all a formality.
"You can," is what I said.

So what started as just me and Gunther turned into ten of us altogether if you counted the horses and you counted the dog. My cook pot was large enough to work for us all, but my tent was on the cramped side. My granny and great aunt had made it from some patchy old canvas my dead great uncle had used to cover hay. They'd calculated the size for me and Frank and Calvin to take out hunting because that's what we'd told them we needed a tent to do.

With an Irish lady in it, though, and her full-grown Mexican boyfriend along with Belle, a runty Pawnee, a fellow from Louisiana and me, that tent could get more than a little close whenever rain caught up with us. Otherwise we'd sleep outdoors beside our fire.

There were times I had some space to myself—usually off in the scrub on my business—when I'd attempt to organize a future for me in my head that still included California and a strike of nuggets and flake. Maybe not enough for a house and fine woman but something at least worth walking halfway across the world about. Then there were other occasions out there when I couldn't tell what we were up to because today looked just like yesterday and tomorrow promised the same.

For a while there, when we'd see people or get hints some were about, we'd have to make Ira scarce in case his reputation had traveled and folks were thinking he'd killed a raft of fellows with a bush axe and a blunderbuss. People clearly preferred their desperados desperate and capable of all grades of ghoulish stuff, but the farther we got from Deakins, the more regular they became. Which is to say Christian and loud about it. There weren't many folks out there who kept the sweet Lord to themselves.

We suffered them all and were grateful for the ones who were gracious and decent and tried to live as examples of everything the good book had told them to be. That sort wasn't common, but we did share the trail with two dozen of them from Boston who'd come out on the plains determined to serve as lights unto the darkness. They were more than ok for the best part of a week.

They shared their food with us, and we only needed to sit through a quarter hour of grace, and they didn't mind at all that Ira was brown and Arturo was Mexican, though it turned out Ira was a funny sort of Catholic, a brand they have in Louisiana, so those Boston Christians mounted an effort to shake him out of that.

Ira made a show of yielding a little, even let those folks pray over him and douse him with some water, but that was chiefly to get to their cornbread and the stews they made with their salt beef, all of it better than what we usually managed in my pot. So we probably would have hung on with them far longer than we did if they'd not confided to us that they were out there to help save savages from burning in the bowels of hell for all eternity.

We tried to tell them to stick with white folks and assured them there were ample heathens about, all stripes of semi-civilized people in danger of burning as well. But they'd made up their minds on a mission to save (most especially) the Sioux and Comanches.

Nobody sought my opinion but I gave it anyway. "They're sure to leave most of y'all dead."

I shared with them the story of how exactly I'd managed to meet up with Belle, and I made sure not to leave out any of the ghastly details. Folks all cut to pieces, shot with guns and shot with arrows, most all of them not just butchered but also scalped. My goal was to tell them far more than they were equipped or willing to hear, but I couldn't seem to get grisly enough to change their minds even a little.

I remember coming that very day to my own religious understanding. Those people were bound to go forth and save the fallen or die in the attempt. One, for them, was just as good as the other. That's why I couldn't scare them off with talk, no matter how unsavory, because death out there among the savages made do for a reward.

So sensible folks were wise to keep clear of missionaries and zealots out in that part of the world. They were only ever on their way to meet their sainted Maker and so weren't likely to be tempted to take care.

Consequently, we told them we were off to visit Arturo's people in Mexico and left that bunch after one last night of cornbread and stew. They blessed us all as we departed, even our homely dog, our mule and ponies. They were generous that way, and I remember watching them wave us off while picturing in my head the pack of them left to the buzzards.

We walked three days north and then turned west. That's when we started seeing something that looked like mountains up ahead. Not actual mountains exactly like the sort I knew back home but glorified hills (I'll call them) lifting modestly out of the plains.

There was a notch in one of them a bit left of cen-

ter, and Ira pointed at it and told us, "Rocky Ford's up
through there."

"You saying you know where you are?" It just kind of
popped out.

Ira looked at me like he needed to and asked me back,
"Don't you?"

3

ven for hills, they weren't all that high, but most everything else was flat, so standing on top we got a decent view of where we'd been and a bit of a look at where we might be going.

I say "might" because the bunch of us had just been traveling along ever since we'd left those Cheyennes behind, that pair of Swedish marauders, and had gotten clear of Deakins with their hanging candidate in tow. We were kind of the human equivalent of something you pick up on your boot—sticky parts and crusty parts and the odd, mysterious nugget—and I was the only one who'd been aiming to end up some place all along. Everybody else had chiefly been leaving where they were. I couldn't be sure any of them had thought too much about where they were going.

Or maybe they just hadn't let me know and were wait-ing for an invitation, so I gave them one that evening after we'd set up our hilltop camp and were sitting around the fire.

"Still figure I'm heading for California," is how I opened it up. "Guessing I'll work a claim."

Nobody looked surprised to hear it or all that interest-ed either. They were just shoving their beans around and probably wishing for cornbread and stew.

"What are y'all thinking?" is what I tried next. I hated to have to take charge, but I've always been the sort who needs to plan and do some forward thinking, which was how me and Frank and Calvin first got organized to come. It was also why it fell to me to make the trip alone because they weren't the sort to honor the details. I'd been getting the sense the bunch I was with weren't all that particular either.

Belle and I, of course, had already come to an under-standing. She'd stick with me, and in exchange for letting her toot and snort as she pleased, I'd get warned about hazards on the trail like savages and vipers. That was a bargain I was happy to make. If she found safe harbor somewhere and wanted me to leave her, my end of things was that I surely would.

I had no such arrangement with any of the others and needed to know what they were thinking.

Since Ira was newest among us, I turned to him so he'd go first. I figured he had the least attachment and so would probably drop off soon.

"Ain't yet been to California," he said and spooned some beans.

"Long way." I pointed what I decided was west.

Ira looked up at the stars to find actual west before pointing somewhere else. "Got a brother heading for Abilene, though. Might ought to meet him there but just as soon hang with y'all for a while."

Arturo took a turn for him and Orla both, announced they'd heard that San Francisco was a town where even Mexicans were taken as they came and people couldn't spare much interest in who a lady loved, even an elegant white one with strawberry blonde hair and freckles.

That sounded awfully fanciful to me, a spot you'd read about in books but have to cross an ocean or two to find.

That only left the Pawnee boy, and between Orla and Arturo, they managed to make him understand the question going around: Was he good with us, or was there somewhere else he wanted to be.

He did some thinking on it and a little wandering as well. He left where we were and went off in the dark to indulge, I guess, in a spot of Indian contemplation. He did some chanting out there and came circling back when he said a lot of stuff in Pawnee and then went off on a wander again.

Orla translated as best she could. "Something about an eagle and a bear."

I'd come to believe it was the Indian way to be windy and deliberate when they weren't filling folks with arrows and carving off patches of hair. If you caught an actual Indian in something like repose and asked him almost any sort of question, he'd weigh it halfway to doomsday and back before he'd come out with only *yes* or *no*.

That Pawnee boy finally showed back up and made a declaration. I could tell because he raised his hands while he was talking to us, and that almost always meant the boy was airing his considered judgment, though on occasion he'd do it when he had a need to go off in the scrub for some relief.

Fortunately, there at the campfire, we were only getting a declaration, and, in fact, it came to us sounding more touching than I would have guessed. Orla did the translating.

"He says he's going with us. He says we're his family now."

I thought one of us needed to say something back, to acknowledge that Pawnee boy's commitment. Since I was the overall instigator and organizer by default, I came out with about the only Pawnee word I knew.

"*Asakis*," I told him and then said it again. Orla reminded me that was the word for dog, which explained why that Pawnee boy went sullen until I'd gone over to take his hand.

I doubt that evening on the hilltop stuck with everybody else or meant as much to them as it meant to me. They probably weren't hungry to hear everybody's plans and their intentions, might even have expected that folks would peel off wherever and whenever they pleased, but I've come to understand that I'm not built the way most people are and require more in this life to be laid plain before me than is common.

So learning we weren't just assorted people traveling the
same direction but were instead something more on the
order of a tribe proved valuable to me and satisfying. With
regular people, I'd have my limits and lines I'd need to
draw, but that wouldn't do if, as the Pawnee boy said, we
were a kind of bunch.

I didn't get moist about it. I knew in my bones we were
more like a gang. I'd call it something between regular,
Christian people and those marauding Swedes. We'd do
what was needed to keep us all safe, and our bond got
tested straightoff once we'd arrived in Rocky Ford, which
was little more than a trading post with an army fort up
the way.

We chiefly needed salt and coffee, and me and Orla
went in for it while the rest of them waited down by a
creek where Gunther and the ponies could drink. Aside
from the clerk, there was a soldier in the store and a couple of dusty cowboys who all gave the eyeball to Orla like
they'd never seen a woman before.

They'd almost certainly never seen a woman like her.
She was fair and pretty, as fit as a boy, had thrown over her
new husband to take up with a Mexican, and had picked
off a pair of savages at full gallop. Those fellows were all
giving Orla the leisurely up and down but had no idea
what they were looking at.

"This your sister?" that soldier wanted to know.

I shook my head and gave my order to the clerk.

"Who is she then?" He'd gone well past eyeballing Orla,
looked primed to lick her if he could.

"Ask her." That was Orla talking.

"All right, darling." He showed his adenoids off. "What you doing way out here?"

"Traveling," she said.

"Not like he'll keep you safe."

I caught myself fingering the grip of my pistol. I'd read and heard all about gunfights, and I could see that soldier had a flap on his holster with a button he'd need to undo. Then I wondered if I could suffer for having defended a woman's honor. If that was a thing, out there in Rocky Ford, I could see a noose about. Every scrap of that went through my head in probably four seconds, but I soon learned Orla didn't need me to let the air out of a man.

She uncorked a snort Belle would have been proud of and asked the clerk about some sort of lady thing. So all that soldier could do was stand there while he got ignored by Orla and then shift my way so I could ignore him too. That felt a lot better than shooting him and appeared to work almost as well.

Once he'd indulged in an ungentlemanly remark, it was one of those dusty cowboys who called him to account.

"That'll do," is all he said and all he needed to say because his holster had no flap or button, and he looked decidedly like the type who'd fired a fair few rounds into men before.

That soldier muttered, took the bundle he'd been waiting on, and said another rude thing but only outside and halfway to his horse.

Those dusty cowboys apologized to Orla on behalf of menkind generally, which must have left them feeling like they couldn't continue to eyeball her, so both of them swung around my way instead.

One of them had a beard on purpose, a wiry thing that hung halfway down his chest. It had snared some stuff, a twig or two and maybe a bit of breakfast, and he kept combing his fingers through it, but nothing seemed to go anywhere. He was also leaking chaw juice from both corners of his mouth while the other came off as nothing worse than dusty, by which I mean he was tidy otherwise and far easier to look at than his partner.

Fortunately for me, he was the one who did the talking. "Where y'all coming from?" he wanted to know.

I pointed somewhere. "Back east a ways."

"Been through Deakins and that?" he asked me.

I couldn't see the harm in owning up to it.

"You ain't come across a…" He squinted hard before requesting help from his partner. "What did they say he was?"

The man spat towards a bucket against the wall and very nearly hit it. He did a poor job of wiping his mouth with his knuckles before he said back, "Octoroon."

"Yeah, one of them," the neat one said to me and then brought out some folded handbills from the pocket of his vest. He opened them flat and sorted through them before offering up to me the one he wanted me to see.

The thing had a likeness of Ira on it, a drawing done with ink, and word that he was worth sixty dollars cash. By then greater Deakins must have given up on the hanging, because he could be brought in dead or alive, whichever suited your needs. The drawing didn't much look like Ira. The fellow on the handbill was three shades darker with a flat nose and considerable lips. He'd killed two men and had rustled horses. They'd listed four names for him. Two of them sounded African. One was Theodore and the other Dematt.

"What exactly," I asked those cowboys together, "is an octoroon?"

The neat one deferred to the one with the beard who said, "Well," and then spat and wiped again. "Like that there," he told me and pointed and at the handbill I was holding, "but maybe not so niggery."

Sometimes people make it easy for you if you wait them out and let them. "Naw," I told them. "Between here and Deakins, didn't see nobody at all."

"How about you?" the neat one asked Orla as an excuse, chiefly, for looking at her. I could tell by the way he never got so far up as her neck.

"I was with him. Saw what he saw."

"Got any Swedes in there?" I asked him.

He shoved his batch of handbills at me, and I went through the bunch myself. He had a Swede but they were calling him Oscar, and he was only worth eighteen dollars. In the drawing, he was mostly beard and eyes. It said on the bill he'd done a killing, but they were considering it manslaughter because the victim had been a lawyer.

"Seen him," I said of Oscar and kind of pointed somewhere again.

But for only eighteen dollars, those two fellows couldn't care.

"Ready?" Orla asked me.

I was more than that and nodded.

"Ira," she told me out in the road, "is nothing like an octoroon."

So they had him too black in the drawing and too white in the description, but people even his general color weren't so common where we were, so we knew we needed to take good care and get well clear of Rocky Ford.

We took the path down where Arturo and them were messing in the water. Even the Pawnee boy had gone waist deep and was rinsing off some grit. Ira, for his part, had gotten his head wet and was trying to make his hair do something while Belle was standing out in the raw sunlight looking pre-premonition to me.

I'd been around enough to have developed a sense of when she was about to go off. She'd get quiet and still in a special way. It was nothing anybody else would notice, but I'd been paying attention long enough to be sensitive and aware. She'd let her arms hang loose with her palms turned out, and she'd look off toward the horizon, but you could tell she was paying her notice to something in her head instead.

I'd been around her enough by then to not even need the alarm she'd raise once whatever she'd been sniffing out was just about to happen.

"Something's up," I told Orla as we reached the stream bank. "I'd probably get the rifle."

Part of being in our sort of family meant you didn't buck and quarrel. If one of us suggested you do a thing, that's exactly what you did. So Orla went straight to Gunther's pack, and she pulled out that old Winchester and checked the rounds.

Arturo noticed. Pawnee boy did too and came up out of the creek. Ira was new enough to us to not know what to make of the charge in the air. He could see that things had crisped up for no conspicuous reason, and he had a look around before he asked us, "What?"

"Ran into some boys," I told him. "They think you did a lot more than you said."

"Does it matter?" he asked me. "Haven't I been all right with y'all?"

In this world now, a question like that wouldn't speak well of a man because of how neat and orderly things have gotten, how clear our duties have become. Back then out there, you sort of had to make your rules as you went. That's what everybody did. There was some law around to reel in the dogged offenders, but lots of killing came off as unavoidable and just. Nobody much got strung up for stuff they could explain away by saying they'd just been holding their ground and keeping themselves or their people safe. Most of the ones who swung were hopeless trash and unpersuasive.

It wasn't fair, and it wasn't consistent, but it was life out there on the ground. So I didn't just want the truth from Ira but needed from him a story that would either convince me he hadn't killed two men and made off with their horses or that he'd needed to and what he'd done was right.

"You've been fine," I told him. "How'd you come to be locked up?"

I could tell he understood I was requesting a revision, and maybe he sensed things would be better for him if he came out true and clear. He had to think about it though, and I let him take his time because there was still nothing to see but red-dirt bluff and sky.

"Money," he said. "Wasn't a thing but that. They owed me and wouldn't pay it, said they didn't need to pay it because of who and what I was."

"Y'all fought?"

He nodded. "Cousins was the bossman. His horse bucked up and threw him. I had nothing to do with that. He busted his arm, and I even tried to help him. I swear that's all, but Overby thought I was up to something else. He was a son-of-a-bitch. Always treated me worse than a dog."

According to Ira, this Overby was a little too loaded to shoot straight, but that didn't keep him from letting the bullets fly.

"Didn't even have my own gun. Took Cousins' off of him, and I told Overby to leave off, but he wouldn't. I shot at him twice. Hit him once." Ira huffed and snorted. "Never seen anything like it. What a mess that made."

"And the horses?" I asked him.

"Took off. Indians probably got them. I don't know why they laid that on me. I walked all the way to town."

"You turned yourself in?"

He nodded. "I thought they'd listen. Some of them knew me a little, and they sure knew how Overby was."

"Guess that didn't pan out like you figured."

"That's one way of looking at it. Yeah, I shot a man, and the other one died, but it didn't go off like they said."

"You could have told us that right at the first."

He shook his head. "Didn't know you then. Got miles beside you now."

That's when the toot came I'd been expecting, and then Belle clapped her hands twice. She did that sometimes too.

"What's she want?" Ira asked me.

I saw those cowboys up on the bluff. Maybe they'd heard there was a black guy down along the creek or maybe they'd just happened to come out for a look. Either way, there they were looking down at us.

The one with the beard and the chaw shouted, "Who you got there?"

"Nobody," is what I said back.

I suspected they were the kind who, since they were after a black man, would settle for most any one they found. It didn't matter if he was the right one, which Ira happened to be. They were going to come down and grab him no matter what. I figure they'd make some declaration like that soldier with my pony and then kill off Ira the first chance they got so they could sling him over a horse.

"What's the plan?" Arturo asked me.

Orla hardly seemed confused. She was aiming up where those cowboys were and awaiting provocation.

I pulled my Colt and told Arturo, "Don't know yet."

I figured those two would come down, and we'd talk them out of something or we wouldn't. After that, things would go like they needed to go. That wasn't a plan exactly but enough to get me ready. Then afterwards we could either explain what had happened and why or, far more likely, clear out and be fugitives clear to California. I'd come a long way from hoeing potatoes and chopping poplars down.

But they didn't come, those two cowboys. I kept waiting to see them on the path, but they failed to show up, and instead we heard some yelling and some gunfire. Then only gunfire. Then whooping and howling, but not quite Comanche style. I'd been exposed to enough of that to know. This was whiskey-fueled white trash racket, and then we could see the dust rising from horses moving out. The next person who looked down over the bluff was some lady in a hat.

I went up with Arturo to see what all the fuss was about and to try to head those dusty cowboys off and keep them up out of the creek bed. That proved not to be much of a chore since both of them were shot to pieces. The one with the beard and the chaw was hanging on, but the neater one was dead.

The citizens of Rocky Ford, such as they were, had come out once the gunfire stopped, and a couple of them were actively wishing that they had a doctor handy instead of a store clerk and a piano teacher and a blacksmith and a barber, but the nearest doctor, they said, was up in Pueblo, and he was hardly any count. They were talking it through, I think, as a way to let that bearded cowboy know he could probably go on and die.

He neglected to, though, but just moaned and writhed while the lady in the hat held a bottle to his lips and made a bid to drown him in whiskey. That and chaw juice since I could see the plug was still in his mouth.

"Who did this?" I asked just generally.

A couple of those folks directed me to the dead cowboy

in the road. He was sprawled on his back and looked to have mostly been shot up, but he did have a knife sticking out of him. It was a big thing that appeared to have come from the sheath strapped to his leg. That knife had been used to skewer both the cowboy and a desperado handbill.

I tried to read it where it was, but it was flapping too much, so I drew out the knife and snagged that sheet, hardly a thing I would have ever imagined I'd have the stomach to do. But there I was with two shot up cowboys engaged in a spot of light reading. That handbill was for the Goins brothers, and I recalled it from before because the money was good—an even one hundred dollars— and the crimes those brothers had gotten up to weren't anything in the usual way.

They'd killed three men over a herd of goats, had burnt a church down with the organist in it, and then had tried to rob a train but had only succeeded at derailing the thing and causing it to pitch into a deep ravine where the engineer and the fireman died and a carful of passengers ended up in a tree.

They were said to be desperate and frequently drunk.

"This look like them?" I asked the woman in the hat with the whiskey.

She said it was nearly a perfect likeness, which raised in my mind the question of how they could draw the Goins brothers near to life but couldn't get anywhere close to an octoroon.

Arturo did some Catholic signaling over those two cowboys, which a few of the Rocky Ford town folks noticed and cared precious little for.

"Let's go back down," I told him, but first I reached into that dead cowboy's vest pocket and helped myself to all his wanted flyers before we went.

"Just say they're shot," I told Arturo as we came down off the bluff, "or Belle'll have us up there digging graves."

Arturo tried, but he was too full of romance to keep things simple and ended up describing the entire scene with the townsfolk and the gore. Then he relieved me of the bloody handbill with the hole in it where the knife had been and the dark spots where that cowboy's blood had stained and marked the paper.

"These two." Arturo held the handbill up to show off that pair of brothers, and then he pointed up toward the top of the bluff and put on a grim expression before announcing that dead cowboy had seven bullets in him and they'd ripped him up going in and torn him to grim chunks coming out.

I'd seen him. It wasn't like that, but I wasn't colorful and Mexican and hadn't made off with an Irish bride. He went on to make quite a tableaux of the woman in the hat pouring whiskey down the gullet of the shot but living cowboy. Clinging to life he was, according to Arturo who left out the beard with the twigs and mess in it. It was hard to quarrel with him. His choices made for a finer tale.

The trouble was, though, he gave rise to the toot I'd anticipated, so I was on my way to fetch the shovel when Ira put to me a question. He'd been looking over a flyer, the one with his likeness on it, and the thing he wanted to know most was, "Dematt?"

I t's no chore to explain my thinking. We had an
appreciable ways to go and maybe money enough
for beans and fatback, coffee if we didn't hope to
have a cup of it every morning, and sugar only for a little
while. Belle could come up with jackrabbits and the occasional prairie hen whenever the spirit moved her to go off
and work her magic, but we lacked sufficient coin among
us for unforeseen calamities or anything in the way of a
general treat.

That'd be providing, of course, that we were being honest with each other. Or rather that Orla and Arturo were
being completely forthcoming with me. I'd brought out all
the money I had, and I was already down to eleven dollars midway between Deakins and Rocky Ford. They each
claimed to have about as much but failed to show it to me,

so I only knew for sure that Belle was skint and Pawnee boy didn't do money while Ira, who'd been locked up in a barn, was lucky he even had shoes.

So maybe we could put together just past twenty dollars, or possibly we couldn't manage that. That's why I started thinking about what we could do for cash, and that led me to bringing up the Goins brothers.

I'd ended up having to dig two graves in the hardpan of the churchyard at the far end of Rocky Ford. Ira spelled me and helped while Arturo primarily directed the work, and the preacher swung by every now and again to suggest that we go deeper.

They had one of those coffins in Rocky Ford that everybody used. Once you got it over the hole, you'd unhook the bottom, and it would hinge open and drop the body into the grave. Practical for sure but more than a little unnerving.

Belle, naturally, didn't care for the sort of praying the preacher got up to and loosed a regular symphony of toots and snorts until I'd started in over those two dusty cowboys with personal remembrances and invocations of the Lord. I kept a consulting eye on Belle until she looked satisfied, and then me and Ira mostly started filling up holes while Arturo hung around to unload some poetry on us. He apparently had no end of verse that he could draw a breath and quote.

So that first night after we left Rocky Ford, I was too whipped to do much but sleep, but our second evening around the fire I floated a suggestion. I'd been studying the wanted flyers and had that dead cowboy's full assortment in my hand.

"Let's say we come across these two." I showed off the Goins brothers. "Or this one or maybe this one." I held up a couple more. "There's nothing to say we can't cash them in."

"Might be kind of dangerous, them being wanted and all." That struck me as an odd approach from Ira.

"You're wanted," I reminded him.

"Yeah, but it wasn't like they said."

"Maybe that holds for the rest of them. Except these two." By then we had to think they'd undersold the Goins brothers. "We grab them up, take them in, get the reward, and go on."

"Don't you need a badge or an order from a judge?" Orla wanted to know.

"Those two back there didn't have them."

"Got to think," Ira said, "they won't want to be grabbed."

"That's where the dead or alive comes in." I'd killed a Comanche. Orla had sort of killed two with an assist from the Pawnee boy, so it wasn't like we had no experience, even if it was only savages. I announced I was convinced I could shoot most things on two feet. "Especially this sort," I said and handed those flyers around for everybody.

"I thought we were going to California." That came my way from Arturo.

"Still are," I told him and tried to sell bounty hunting as an efficiency we might get up to along the way.

I got the clear sense nobody much shared my enthusiasm until Orla pulled me aside the following morning and suggested we stop in Pueblo to find the sheriff or the marshal and take every kind of flyer he might have.

I didn't know at the time if those two Indians she'd shot off their horses were the first two men of any kind she'd killed, but I could tell she'd hardened to the act essentially like I had. You pull the trigger, and then you wait for the guilt and the remorse. They come at you but far weaker than you've been brought up to think, and after a while, you can't even locate a twinge anymore.

Killing wasn't the job before us, though. I was proposing a public service that didn't have to end with a bunch of desperados getting dead. The chances were decent we'd never even see one since we weren't planning to chase them around, but it seemed sensible and efficient to keep yourself ready for any rascals who happened by.

Orla allowed she could appreciate the wisdom in that and then confided in a whisper that she and Arturo had eight and a half dollars between them.

So I'd gained an ally, one prepared to pull a trigger, which left me hoping I could still get Belle on board. My thinking was if I showed her the handbills, she might come by a feel for the desperados, so if we got in the vicinity of any of those boys, she'd let me know with one of her fits. I couldn't be sure that's how her stuff worked, but I also couldn't be sure it wasn't.

Looking back, it all sounds crazy, and I had that business by the wrong end because our group was qualified to be a scoundrel and rascal magnet. We had a girl, a woman, a scrawny Indian, a Louisiana octoroon, a sentimental Mexican, and a boy from the Alleghenies whose best

friend in the world was a mule. And there all of us were
just out in the wild ripe to get ridden up on by men convinced they could use us as they pleased.

We were natural bait, but I couldn't quite see it until a
fellow came along to point it out.

Before then, we took the trouble of hunting a lawman
down in Pueblo where Orla went off with Belle to buy
the pair of them proper baths. Ira and that Pawnee boy
kept up with Gunther and the horses while me and Arturo
tracked the marshal down. He happened to just be back
from up across the Arkansas River where he'd captured a
couple of fellows who'd robbed the overland mail and had
killed the wagon master because that gentleman had been
lippy. That's what the marshal told us because that's what
one of those boys had said to him. The dead one, as it
turned out. He'd brought the other one back just flogged.

Once he'd finished his tale, I asked him, "Can anybody
do that sort of thing?"

"What?"

"Bring thieves and scoundrels in and get paid out?"

"I suppose," he told me, and then talked to me like I
was just some sixteen-year-old-boy who'd be better off
courting and planting a garden or maybe running cattle.

"You don't want to mess with this," he said. "They'll all
be looking to kill you first."

So I shifted around and came at it another way. That
was a technique I'd discovered a talent for along the trail.
I'd meet with some kind of barricade and instead of hammering at it, I'd search out a way around the thing no
matter how wide I needed to go.

"Let's say we're out there," is how I put it, "and a boy or three rides up on us. If we've studied those flyers, maybe we know what we're in for and don't have to fool around to find out who we're dealing with." Then I brought up the Goins brothers and the near miss we'd had with them. "I want to think well of my fellow man, but…" I gave him a snort I'd learned from Belle.

"Well," he said, "All right, I guess." He rounded up flyers for us and handed the stack of them, naturally, to Arturo because he was a grown man even if I was the one who'd killed a Comanche and was scarring up inside.

There must have been twenty of those handbills altogether, and only a couple of them were repeats of flyers we already had.

When Ira saw that stack, he said, "Nobody much does right out here."

That was certainly one way to look at it, but I took a slightly different view. It was more that people got in situations that usually included a couple of guns. Back home, we'd have all kinds of tussles and bloody disagreements, but if you wanted to bring a rifle into it, you'd have to go home and fetch it. By then you might have thought of something else you needed to do.

Out where we were, with a Colt Navy on your hip or Winchester shoved down by your saddle, you lacked the need for brainwork, and the bullets tended to fly.

So, yes, there were plenty of people who didn't do right out there, but I laid the blame primarily on too many violent options.

Once Orla and Belle had come back clean but in their

dirty clothes again, we left Pueblo and soon enough were seeing a ridgeline to the west high enough to make me hunt around for my buffalo hide hat.

That night and nights beyond it, we all studied those wanted flyers and made ourselves acquainted with the various features of those men. And they were all men, even though one of them dressed up sometimes like a lady so he could go into banks and raise no alarm at first. Two of them were missing parts of their ears, and one of them wore an eyepatch, while the guy known only as Hassip had six fingers on his left hand.

We made kind of a game out of it and would pass the time by quizzing each other on the trail and around the fire. Who had the scar under his bottom lip? Who had the birthmark shaped like Tennessee? Which one walked with a limp because he'd fallen down a shaft, and what of that bunch had gotten half scalped but lived to tell about it? Those boys had no end of markers and acutely distinguishing features, and it soon came to be an unpleasant thing to meet with us on the trail because we'd give every pilgrim we saw a comprehensive scour and quiz them on stuff only our flyer boys would know.

None of it got us any closer to a cash reward until we'd reached that string of mountains and passed through a gap into a valley where we pitched camp in a beauty spot in with some evergreens by a creek. It was damp back there, so we'd built a sizable fire when a couple of white men came walking up. They were leading four good-looking horses.

One of them was wearing a suit of clothes like you'd get

married in, but they were dusty and wrinkled. His shirt-front had frills that had largely given up. I immediately took against his mustache because he openly and per-sistently cared about it too much.

The other one was a weaselly sort. Everything about him was filthy. It was certainly a chore to stay clean out there, but you could do it if not being nasty was a goal. I wouldn't have cut a fishing worm in half with his finger-nails out of consideration for the worm.

"Hey, y'all," the one with the mustache told us.

By then, I was working (and probably the rest of them too) through the features of all the men on the flyers that we'd accumulated. These two certainly impressed as sorry and hardly looked the kind to have come by twice as many horses as they needed in an honest way.

I left Arturo to do the talking. He was a good one for that job because he had a talent for chat but was Mexican, so we could see if that provoked them. Some of the fellows we'd studied had killed a few Mexicans in the general course of their carnage, but they usually didn't make it to a handbill unless they'd gunned down white folks too.

"Gentlemen," Arturo said. "How go your travels?"

Those two weren't big on small talk. One of them responded by stroking his mustache, while the nasty one pointed toward our campfire and asked anybody who'd care to tell him, "Beans?"

I noticed he did everything with his right hand. He was holding two sets of reins with it, scratched himself with it when that was required, and pointed out our beans with it as well. His left arm just hung there. I waited for him

to use it, and I saw when he turned it swung free like a
knotted rope.

The sight of that sparked me up a little, and I went
sifting through some desperado details in my head because
I felt like one of those wanted men was suffering from arm
trouble—had a shrunken arm or a stunted arm or an arm
shot up and left useless. I couldn't recall exactly which it
was and wished instead he had a birthmark shaped like
Tennessee.

"Want some?" Ira asked that fellow and stepped over to
the pot. He stirred our beans and picked up a bowl for our
guest.

"Where you from, boy?" the nasty one asked Ira.

I could feel the air change all of a sudden, like there
was lightning in it. I'd already decided if those two were
accomplished at whatever they were up to they almost
certainly wouldn't look like they did. One of them had
reduced all his vanity to a mustache that he was working
overtime to keep tidy and presentable, while the other one
appeared to have quit on everything but food.

I went to reach for my Colt, just lay my hand on it,
but there wasn't any gun to find because I'd taken it off
already. You couldn't really sit around on the ground with
something like that on your hip. So even after all the study
and all the preparation, I was at the mercy of those boys. I
guessed we all were, and those two seemed to notice it as
well because they glanced at each other before the weaselly
one pulled out his revolver. A buntline, I guessed. It was
about the longest pistol I'd ever seen.

He grinned as he drew it, and his teeth were worse than

his fingernails. I remember thinking I hated to die at the hands of such a nasty human, but I didn't get the chance to dwell on it because Orla shot the boy dead.

She was cagier than the rest of us, was for sure far sharper than me, so she'd taken her Smith and Wesson with her when she went to sit for supper. Being a woman, I guess, she knew that louts could always be around and so was ready for these two to come up out of the woods.

That nasty fellow took an interest in the hole the bullet made. He had a careful look at it before he sank to his knees with a groan while the other one finally gave up long enough on mustache grooming to produce a Derringer from somewhere up his arm. That made perfect sense for him. He looked the sort who'd cheat at poker, but he was out of the saloon, and the shot he got off only hit the ground and spooked the dog.

I'm sure Orla would have plugged him too if he'd not scampered in such a way to put a horse directly between her and him. He left all four of them behind and lit out through the woods in just his dirty, fancy suit. He even dropped his hat. It was a nice one, and I handed it over to Ira who'd been getting along with just a rag on his head.

That hat had the fellow's name scratched in the band— LJ Burke—and that was enough to ring some bells for the whole bunch of us.

"His didn't say nothing about a mustache," I was announcing by way of excuse when Orla volunteered her view that we'd be foolish to leave him wandering since we had all their horses with all their stuff, and he just had a dirty suit and a gun that shot two rounds.

"Nothing else?" I asked her.

Orla pointed at a double rig hanging off one of the horses. That fellow had gone off and left a pair of bone-handled smokewagons behind.

I'd taken hard against LJ Burke, chiefly for the moustache, but I also couldn't think terribly much of a man who'd run with the boy we'd put down. Just then Arturo began to read out the crimes and the personal details on Mr. L.J. Burke's wanted flyer.

He'd killed a man in a saloon in Cimarron, Kansas. He'd shot him over a gambling debt the man was refusing to pay. Burke was also thought to have killed a livery boy with a blow to the head, and he was wanted for the malicious wounding of a Delaware Indian with a knife. There was some thieving thrown in there was well and a solitary assault on a woman. He'd not ravaged her but had taken against the woman for unknown reasons, and in a fit of pique, Burke had knocked her down.

LJ Burke was known to ride with a towheaded boy called Finch, and he'd been seen in the company of a Crowder from Dakota who was described as "slight" and "grimy." Only by way of an afterthought was mention made of his useless arm.

I felt like the lesson for me was that I needed to read a lot closer. Orla wasn't ready to wonder about that yet because Burke was still loose in the woods.

"Before we lose the light," she told me and went off after him with the rifle. I strapped on my Colt and joined her in the pines while Ira and Arturo each grabbed a smokewagon and waited where they were in case he circled back.

It was dim in the woods and hard to see, but we hadn't gone more than thirty yards when we heard ground clutter crunching, and I soon caught sight of a few of the frilly bits of LJ Burke's fancy shirt.

He showed us both of his hands and started talking. "I'm thinking we can work something out," he said.

It seemed wise just then to let Orla do our negotiating since she'd been the one to lay Burke's partner low.

"Like what?" she asked him.

"I just need one horse. The rest of it's yours to have."

"It's already ours to have," she told him.

He laughed. "I'm going to come up a little." He walked our way, his hands still raised, though he'd let them droop a bit.

"Have pity on a fellow traveler," is what he told us next. "Why?"

Orla was being far flintier than I knew I would have been. I could readily shoot a whooping Comanche closing on me with a knife, but I had qualms about white men in wedding suits. It was nothing I was thinking through. I just felt myself going easier on him because he looked like a lot of fellows I might have seen around.

Thinking back, that's probably precisely the view that Orla took as well. Being a woman, though, she'd probably had a poorer time with men. So while LJ Burke was earning favor with me, he was yielding it up with Orla.

"Now, darling…" He let his hands fall, and I guess he might have been reaching for something. He probably was hoping to soften up Orla while he made his move. He let on she had a lot of spine for such a pretty thing, but she'd shot him already before he could really get going.

"He would have been nothing but trouble," she told me. Then the rest of our crew came running in.

He did have a bullet in his derringer, which was part way up his sleeve, and there was a knife of butchering size slipped down in one of his boots. So you could more than make a case that he was angling to be a problem, and I let that be enough to satisfy me.

I would become quite a lot easier to satisfy as we moved along, but none of us would ever fully catch up with Orla who couldn't tolerate getting explained at by a man, getting told how this world should operate and how things ought to go and that a pretty thing like her ought to set her rifle down. It was the sort of talk that often launched with *now, darling* or *aw, sugar* and ended almost invariably with a corpse.

The four of us men carried Burke's body in to lay it by his partner's, after which we picked off of them anything that seemed of use. Arturo took the derringer. Ira made do with Burke's hat and boots, and the man was carrying a California gold piece and eighteen dollars in scrip. I gave all of that to Orla to keep and then had a think with Arturo and Ira on how best to truss those dead guys up for draping on a horse.

Ira had been on boats and knew some knots. We had little rope but plenty of leather tack, which worked well enough, and we got those two bound up and ready in probably a half hour, and then the bunch of us ate our supper like nothing had gone on.

Come morning, we turned around and headed back to

Pueblo. The marshal we'd talked to sure looked surprised to see us, especially hauling two dead men trussed up like Christmas geese.

I handed him the flyer with LJ Burke's likeness on it.

"It's him and Crowder," I told him. "They came up on us in the woods. Didn't really pan out like they'd hoped."

The marshal compared LJ Burke to his handbill sketch and then pulled a face once he'd leaned in to inspect Burke's nasty running buddy.

Orla informed him, "Smelled like that alive."

"All right," he said and checked the handbill. "That's fifty for the pair. Let's see if I've got it."

With that, he went into the jailhouse and came straight back out with cash that he tried to give to Arturo because, even if he was a Mexican, Arturo was the thing we had closest to a regular man. He pointed though, along with the rest of us, Orla's way instead, and she took the money and thanked the marshal for it.

"We'd kind of like to keep their pistols," I said, "and maybe one of their horses."

He'd called deputies out to wrangle the bodies. "Go on," he told me back.

So we took what we wanted, traded off Arturo and Orla's Cheyenne pony, and then hung around while Orla took Belle with her to buy some useful clothes, the kind that rough and ready frontier women needed. They came back dressed like a couple of boys. Trousers instead of skirts. Shirts instead of blouses. And proper wide-brimmed hats to keep them clear of the sun. They'd bought blankets as well to help see us over the snowy mountains and biscuits you didn't need the teeth of a wolf to eat.

The marshal saw us off from in front of the jail with Burke and Crowder laying on the plank walk at his feet.

"Ain't y'all a bunch," he told us. He whistled once and shook his head.

A Mexican, an Indian, a woman and a girl, an octoroon from Louisiana, a glorified boy from the Alleghenies. We were on our way to being a bunch all right.

The Woman
and the Goat

1

We made like we were still headed west and aiming for California, but we didn't move out with any dispatch and spent time veering south and north. At first, we didn't talk in any direct way about what we were up to, but a group like ours could only dawdle without comment for a while. It was like we weren't prepared to fully break from the pull of Pueblo because we knew that's where the marshal and the payout money was.

Once you've taken good money for delivering men you didn't feel a thing about, doing it another time can start to grab you like a calling. That's what was going on, but didn't any of us say until after two weeks had passed by, and we'd all but circled Pueblo, had gone on sallies north and south but had spent most of our time on the overland

trail where we'd met with a slew of people. We talked to
more folks after Burke and Crowder than I'd seen since
leaving home.

But we still didn't own up to what we were doing in any
direct and honest way until that Pawnee boy put all sorts
of questions to Orla and Arturo. He wasn't, for an Indian,
anything like gifted with directions. He could go thirty
feet into the deep woods and about get lost coming back. I
think that's especially why he missed the regular company
of his dog since the dog always knew where they were.

But even that Pawnee boy could tell we were on some
kind of wander and were looping back to places we'd
traveled through before. He wanted to know what we were
up to and said it was his people's custom to move straight
from place to place to place to place. At the end of the line
they'd sometimes turn around and do it backwards, but he
declared we seemed to be up to something far more aim-
less than that.

He said it all to Orla and Arturo who put it in English
for us, and I was primed with a comment of my own because I'd been mulling too.

"We're on the scour, aren't we?" I aimed that at Orla.
"I'll be thinking tomorrow we'll go on west, but we keep
on hanging back."

"Gift horse and that," was Orla's response.

It wasn't like we had gotten together and had anything
like a chat. Instead, we were only mindful there were
wanted men around and a town within striking distance
where we could cash them in.

"Take a vote maybe," was my suggestion.

So at camp there one evening we gathered for what could have passed for a prayer meeting, and Orla even let Arturo open the thing with a Mexican poem. It was, naturally, about both the rigors of fate and a tragic, heartbroken woman. Those were the twin staples of Mexican poetry as best I could tell. Also, it all went on for longer than I'd like a poem to go, and it didn't help it was in Spanish and Orla was only half translating because she seemed to have reached her limit with Arturo's poetic side.

They were an evermore curious pair, those two. Arturo was large and swarthy and dashing while Orla was slight and pale and came off meek, and yet he was the one who could see a field of flowers and go aquiver while she was shooting Comanches off their ponies and gunning down men in the woods. Arturo was weak against beauty. Orla was weak against cash and didn't much care if she had to be trigger happy to get it.

She allowed Arturo to wind up and very nearly finish his poem before Orla spelled out what had become even obvious to our Pawnee. "I'm convinced," she said, "there's money to be made."

I wasn't above cashing in as well. I'd come all that way fairly ignorant of even the mechanics of gold mining. Because I was prepared to squat in a California creek and eyeball loads of silt didn't at all mean I was likely to make much of it. So I was open to an alternative, though something more organized than I'd lately seen. Up to that point, we'd only been milling around in the vicinity of Pueblo. That didn't feel much like a strategy to me.

Orla plainly had been doing a good bit of mulling herself and had put together in her head a plan for us going forward that kept us chiefly to the wagon road between Pueblo and Breckenridge, a town a hundred miles north on a trail up through a valley. It was a mining spot, supply depot, and watering hole for scoundrels. That's what Orla had picked up in Pueblo from being pretty and listening out.

So we'd head north in no big hurry and talk to people along the road to find out what they'd heard about the lowlives we were after. Details about the exploits of thieving trash spread like the pox out there.

"We try it a while," was Orla's suggestion. "If nothing comes of it, we move on along."

That made sense since we'd be north already and could go on over the mountains on a route most people took. So we voted, all of us but for the dog and Gunther, and made it official.

Things felt different right away because we didn't avoid people, most especially the first four we met up with who were rowdy because they were drunk and yet still in the saddle somehow. They were headed to Pueblo for women and seemed ready to make us a waypoint if Orla would oblige. We didn't have to shoot any of them. They weren't sufficiently focused for that and turned on Orla once they had established she was Irish and content to be in the company of a Mexican, an Indian, and an octoroon. They even took time out to insult the dog.

They weren't worth any reward at all, but we still half wanted them dead. That suggested to me that cozying up to people might be a challenge for us with people being generally what they were.

At first, we let Arturo serve as our ambassador because he had kind eyes and a winning smile, but they weren't enough to compensate for the fact he was a Mexican. Most of the people we came across were more than willing to let us know they didn't care for Mexicans much at all. They didn't like Indians either and had little use for Negroes. It made no difference to them our particular Negro was something like an octoroon.

That part of the world at that time didn't hold much pull for polite people, or at least the sort who could detest anybody who wasn't white and still give you a thin smile and keep it to themselves. Out where we were, people spoke up. A steady diet of whisky helped or a sense of burning purpose. Those Bible folks in particular said all kinds of rotten things. They seemed to have decided that Jesus liked it when they opened up.

And yet Orla failed to squeeze off a single shot, and we didn't fall on anybody and beat them senseless because we all knew we had a job to do out there on the wagon road.

We had a taste of success after less than a week of chatting up whoever we met. A woman out there near some trading stop that went by the name of Guffey said her brother had gotten waylaid by a gang of boys not three days back.

She described the scar down one of them's cheek, and that rang a bell with us because we had a flyer for a Winthrop whose leading feature was a scar like that. He told people he'd gotten it from a sword when he'd charged the rebs at Antietam, but that seemed unlikely since he would

have been six years old or something close. The truth was
he'd come off of his horse and landed face-first on a rock.
He'd gotten help in that from a cousin of his who was
beating him with a shovel. We'd heard that story from the
marshal in Pueblo who'd known this Winthrop before he
was trash.

"Came from fine people," was the way he told it to us,
by which he meant folks he'd not been obliged to hunt
down and arrest even once. "Fine people" on the frontier
would get run out of Richmond or New York.

That lady on the trail told us where to find her brother.
He had a homestead and a wife and couple of kids just up
the way. I went with Orla to talk to him because she was
pretty and Irish while I was ordinary and white, and we'd
picked up even by then who was a provocation and why.

That gentleman was still puffy from having taken a
punch or six, and he had reason to believe those boys were
out by a place called Antelope Hole.

"Got whores over there," he told us both and then
apologized to Orla, partly for not calling them ladies and
partly for what they sprawled on beds and did. He said he
would have gone out there and killed them himself but
had a mess of pigs to see after and a wife he'd hate to leave
in a fix.

We just listened mostly. He needed to let out the shame
and the anger over having been beat up. Robbed too, of
course. He'd lost a pony, a Sharps Carbine he'd come by
from his daddy, and the worst of it was they'd even made
off with his brand new dungarees.

He wanted to hear about whatever quarrel we had with

that Winthrop, and instead of telling him we were carrying paper and hoping for a reward, Orla spun him a tale about a tangle we'd had with the boy and a number of sentimental personal items he'd filched from us.

Antelope Hole was off the wagon road about six miles and was mostly just a fort the army had half built and then quit on. They'd moved somewhere else and left the place to whoever came along, which turned out to be an enterprising woman named Roticia who had two husbands she was dragging around by an accident of fate. She'd married the second one because the first one had died up in the Yukon but not so thoroughly, as it turned out, that he couldn't locate her again.

We heard all of this from Roticia herself. That'd be me and Arturo, who told her we were on the prowl for a couple of sporting women, and he showed Roticia money enough to head her off from caring that he was a Mexican and I was only a boy.

We were in her receiving room. All of her customers were obliged to pass through there to the bunk house. That's what it had been anyway before Roticia dressed it up and filled it with girls. Or before, anyway, her husbands had worked a renovation on the place. It turned out the dead one and the live one were both handy and got along well for two men married to exactly the same woman.

When Yukon husband showed back up, he confessed that he'd taken an arctic Indian for a wife because he couldn't figure out any other way to get himself sheltered and fed while he was stuck way up there waiting for the thaw.

Roticia informed him she'd done the same thing, just down in Kansas territory where she'd locked in her food and a roof above her through a gentleman named Bob. So she guessed they were even, and Yukon could put up with Bob or head back north. Yukon was tired of seal meat and the penetrating cold and decided he could stand being part of a couple with Roticia and Bob.

So that was the team that refit the half-built fort Roticia bought at a government auction for hardly more than a couple of dollars. Then she hired on a pack of sporting women for men on the wagon road who didn't mind traveling a few miles wide for something like romance at a fee well south of Pueblo city prices. From what I saw, the women weren't up to city standards either. Not homely necessarily but practical like farm girls. They did what was needed to men who came through like they'd do what was needed to cows.

We talked to a trio of them in the reception room where we stalled by making like we were picky with odd stuff we required. I left that mostly to Arturo since I had limited experience with girls, by which I meant I'd wrestled and tried to kiss one but hadn't come away any wiser than I'd gone in. Arturo, though, he knew some stuff and acquainted that trio of girls before us with his extensive peccadillos. He was even gracious enough to let me have a few, made me big on feet in a general way and gave me an appetite for doing most of my business standing up.

After a quarter hour of that sort of talk, with Roticia growing impatient, we were about ready to move to the bunkhouse when Winthrop came staggering out. He was wearing brand new dungarees and had pulled on one of his boots. It was impossible not to know him by his scar. He had a handful of money and had come out to trade in his old girl for a fresh one.

"Says she's through," he told Roticia. "Says she's had enough of me."

Roticia didn't like the sound of that. She announced she couldn't tolerate girls who were squeamish and particular, and she went stalking toward the bunkhouse to set a few things straight. That gave us all the elbow room we needed.

"Winthrop," I said since I wasn't Mexican. "What the hell you doing here?"

He turned my way. I could see he was too sloshed with whiskey to focus and just stood with his mouth gaped open gawking at me and Arturo.

"We been looking all over," I told him.

Me and Arturo got up off of the velvet settee we'd been perched on, and each of us grabbed Winthrop by an arm, all smiling and friendly there at first.

He thought he didn't know us, but he couldn't be sure of it, so he just made a few noises as we squired him toward the door, but he'd soon decided he didn't want to go out in just his trousers. Furthermore, while he'd judged that I could possibly be a friend of his, he said he made it policy not to know any Mexicans.

"Who's this José?" he asked us and tried to jerk himself free, so I pulled out my Colt and beat him a little with it. That rendered him agreeable enough for us to drag him on outside.

Orla met us in the dooryard. She had the Winchester in hand while Ira, beside her, was holding our rope because we'd determined to try to take a live one back from the wilds, mostly to find out if it could even be done. Orla was doubtful, but me and Arturo and Ira had convinced her to let us attempt it. In that way, she was like the girls inside—up for doing what was required.

That Winthrop didn't want to be tied up, and he made the mistake of taking Orla for a working woman and guessed she was older than he liked them but he'd give her a go anyway. He managed to get that out clear enough for all of us to hear, and it earned him a rifle butt flush to the forehead. That took all the starch out of him, and I helped Ira truss him up. We soon had him over a horse's back and strapped down so he couldn't move, which I would have counted as a success if his friends hadn't come boiling out just then.

There were three of them, all drunk and all in their long johns, but they'd brought guns with them. One of them had a Sharps Carbine in hand, and the other two didn't wait to hear an explanation but just started shooting their pistols. The fellow with the Sharps Carbine aimed the thing at Belle. She was up on her bay and not ten feet from him. She didn't move. She didn't look anxious. She just tooted, and he missed.

Him, of course, I had to shoot for trying to kill a child while Orla took care of the other two because they were hazards to us, and all the yelling and the gunfire had served to wake that Winthrop up. So he started squirming and wriggling, wailed and hollered quite a lot. Orla was all for dragging him off the horse and shooting him dead too, but I settled him down by hammering on him some more just as Roticia and Yukon and Bob came out to see exactly what was up.

Yukon looked part grizzly bear. He had far more beard than was useful or necessary. Bob, on the other hand, looked like an undertaker. He was tall and bony and had no hair anywhere. They were both holding guns but had the good sense not to point them. Yukon's looked like a musket. Bob had brought out a pepperbox.

"What's all this?" Roticia wanted to know.

Arturo, who kept our paper, showed her the handbill with Winthrop on it.

"And them?" she asked of his three dead buddies.

Arturo mostly shrugged.

"Y'all tidy up." Roticia directed that at husbands Yukon and Bob who, by the way they jumped, appeared to be familiar with that brand of instruction. Roticia couldn't be troubled to linger. She went straight back inside.

"You want them?" Bob asked us.

We weren't altogether sure until we'd inspected each of those boys and had tried to match them with flyers we had. As best we could tell, they were scoundrels the law wasn't hungering after yet.

So we didn't want them, but that was hardly enough to keep Belle from snorting and tooting. I pulled out the shovel and asked Yukon and Bob where we might plant those boys.

Bob fetched a lantern and led us all into the woods and over to a lumpy clearing. He pointed at spots where we wouldn't hit anything they'd buried before.

"Get a lot of this?" I asked him.

Bob yielded to Yukon for a response. "Men go funny sometimes when they have to share a girl."

It looked like they had four men gone funny in that clearing with three more to come, and one of them only died once we got out there. We weren't obliged to hurt him further. He just gave up finally and went.

It all sounds brutal now, savage and bloodthirsty and maybe criminal as well, but that's not how it was back then. You acted one way in civilized places, but out in the countryside, no law applied in any ordinary fashion. If you weren't prepared to meet harm with harm, somebody would have found a clearing to put you in.

So we regretted having taken the lives of three of that Winthrop's buddies, and because of Belle we were doing for them something close to a decent thing, but that was just how life went out there, and usually without the burial and the benediction. It wasn't at all uncommon for people to simply get left where they fell.

Consequently, then, we were being something close to Christian, and Yukon and Bob both noticed that me and Ira (who were doing the digging) were getting directed by a blonde girl with only snorts and toots.

"She don't talk," I told them.

"They cut her tongue out?" Yukon asked. "I've seen people they done that to." He bothered to glance Pawnee boy's way as he said it.

I shook my head. "She's got one but only toots and stuff."

Belle obliged us just then with a sample. She thought the grave we were on was too shallow.

Ira was doing the digging just then and told her straight back, "I ain't done."

I eyed Winthrop's three dead friends on the ground and informed Yukon and Bob, "The girl's got kind of a thing for doing right."

They could appreciate that. They weren't Godly men, and each confessed as much, but they allowed both together that they could see the point of being decent.

"Tried to bury one of mine once," Yukon told us, "but the ground was too damn hard." Then they said they'd heard I had an interest in feet.

Once we'd laid those boys in and I'd prayed enough to make Belle satisfied, we went back to find that Orla and Roticia had collected all the money together that bunch had been carrying with them and had divided it up in a fair and proper way. We took the Sharps Carbine, Winthrop's new dungarees, and three of their horses, including the one that looked like it probably belonged to the beat up homesteader we'd met, and then we went back to the wagon road and turned north away from Pueblo to give that man his gun, his pants, his horse and what was his of the cash.

We didn't decide that's what we'd do. We all just did it without saying, all of us anyway but for Pawnee boy who needed an explanation because he was still working to figure the white man out. If I'm honest, I was doing a spot of that myself. I'd come all that way thinking I'd be a miner, and there I'd killed at least two men, even if one of them was just a Comanche, but it only half felt like the road to perdition because those men had both needed to go. So let's say I was troubled but hardly enough to do anything much about it.

It helped that the guy with the wife and the kids and the pigs was truly grateful, and he let us know he was more than a little surprised and pleased that we'd proved decent.

"You know how folks are," he told us.

We all nodded. We sure did.

That Winthrop needed tapping a time or two while we were on the road back to Pueblo. He'd get loud and wriggly and make trouble for his horse, and I'd hit him with my Colt or Pawnee boy would tap him with a pine knot he'd found. He seemed to welcome the duty of helping to make the trussed up white man quiet and went at it with maybe more enthusiasm than was required. Winthrop, for his part, didn't trouble us much those last few miles into town.

It was mid-morning by the time we finally reached the Pueblo jail house. One of the marshal's men saw us coming and went inside to fetch his boss who stepped out with his coffee and a chicken leg he was scraping clean with his teeth.

"Now who?" he asked.

Arturo handed over that Winthrop's flyer. The marshal looked at the drawing and then made a gesture my way so I'd pick up that Winthrop's head. I grabbed a fistful of hair and showed the marshal his face.

"All right. That's fifty more for y'all. I've got to say, you're making a few of these bounty boys around here ill."

"It's anybody's game." That from Orla.

The marshal pitched his bone into the road. "That's what I told them," he said.

"We get any more for bringing him in alive?" is what I wanted to know.

"Lucky to get as much. It's worse that way. He goes to court."

That was a lesson for us all that we never took pains to discuss, but from then on we all got quicker on the trigger once we'd picked out our man.

Me and Ira and Pawnee boy managed to get Winthrop untied after a while. We didn't want to cut the rope that was holding him wrist-to-ankles because we'd only just bought it, and Ira kept thinking he had his knots free until the horse would shift and tighten them again. So we fooled around long enough for Orla to chew on us. Belle even did some tooting, and Arturo recited three whole poems. But we did work him loose and carried him up on the jailhouse porch where that Winthrop came off as well past groggy.

"Had to knock him on the head," I explained to the marshal. "He got rowdy here and there."

The marshal nodded and shoved that Winthrop a couple of times with his boot before he told me back, "I guess that's why he's dead."

2

We didn't get badges, but we did get certificates. We got one certificate anyway that we were directed to share between us if somebody ever asked us about authority and such. The marshal also gave us a batch of new handbills with a fresh bunch of ne'er do wells on them. It seemed that breaking the law in various ways, most of them bloody and wanton, was an ever-growing course of life out there.

He also warned us about our colleagues, usually men and most in pairs, who wouldn't take kindly to competition from a bunch like us.

"Got a woman," he said, "and a colored, an Indian, a Mexican, a girl. And what are you? Twelve?" he asked me.

I could have pulled my Colt and shot him, but I was

working on being unperturbable and reliably even-hand-
ed. So I just lied and said that I was twenty-three.

"Well," he told me, "they won't like you either, taking
cash out of their pockets and bread out of their mouths."

"Isn't like we'll be quitting," Orla told the marshal.

I think he'd taken kind of a shine to her. He grinned.
"Yeah, figured that."

So we felt like we'd made an ally and had a backer in the
right spot who didn't mind that we were a curious bunch
and sometimes brought in our live ones dead. It was more
that we were trying to be particular and industrious about
it, so if we hauled in some corpses, they'd be the ones that
needed rounding up.

"Dupree especially," was the final thing he said. "He'd as
soon kill you as let you get his man." He said we'd know
him from his Spanish saddle with all grades of tooling on
it, his stubby shotgun, and the top hat he wore that was
too small for his head.

So back north we went on the Breckinridge road, figured we'd stick to it until our luck gave out. We joined a
wagon train for a few days. Half the folks in it were Hungarian, and the rest of them were Irish from some county
back there Orla knew. So she got friendly with them fast
and heard all about the villains and Indians they'd run into
since the river. Most recently they'd fought off some dog
soldiers who'd come at them three dozen strong.

I'd heard about them, Indian delinquents and misfits
from different tribes. Those boys would throw in together
and ride around killing and scalping and stealing. They
were the worst of the worst, bad Cheyenne primarily

but with Sioux dregs and Navajo and even Pawnee trash thrown in. They were on a rampage and were sure to stay at it until the army or some settlers wiped them out.

Pawnee boy did quite a lot of spitting and raging when he heard dog soldiers had lately been around. I'm sure it was hard enough already to be an Indian out in that part of the world without having the bloodthirsty worst of your lot joining up and running wild.

Personally, I appreciated Pawnee boy's irritation because he gave us so few signs of what was going on with him. That made it nice, at least for me, to see him proud of being the kind of Indian who wouldn't just get up to any old thing. Naturally, those Hungarians and the Irish too treated our Pawnee boy poorly, but most people need somebody to look down their noses at. Even foreign folks in a wagon train with all their worldly treasures in a trunk.

We did come away from that wagon train with one useful piece of desperado intelligence. A man had joined up with those people for a couple of days and broken off and left them just before they'd reached the town of Cactus Flats because he said he might know folks there who'd want to do him harm. And that's when he brought out and showed them a wanted flyer with his likeness on it. The law was on him for killing a man and a woman and their pet long-eared goat who he said was part of the tent show they put on. Those two did magic and mind reading while the goat, when called upon, would count to ten.

"Got tangled up with them," that fellow had confessed to some of the wagon train people, "but I didn't do nothing at all to her or the goat."

He said he wanted them to know that in case they heard talk about him later. He seemed persuaded people would up and say any damn thing.

Since we didn't have any paper on him, we got his name and particulars from a couple of those Hungarians. He was a Haskins, and they seemed to remember his proper name was Lloyd, but that didn't matter much because he went by Little Dusty and had explained to those folks Big Dusty was some trashy boy in Texas and they shouldn't be tempted to confuse the two.

So we learned there was an easy payday in the vicinity of Cactus Flats, which was just the kind of information we were after. That made for a worthwhile couple of days, and we'd only just taken our leave of those people when Belle had one of her fits.

The dog sat down. That was our clue because Belle was given to stopping occasionally for no particular reason, but the dog only seemed to drop to his haunches and look up at her on her mount when she was going mystical and peculiar. That was the case on this occasion. Belle sighed and tooted and tooted and sighed. Then she advanced to warbling and shivered a bit before she shifted around to point in the direction we'd just come. We all knew to take that for instruction.

So we turned back and drew up in sight of the wagon train we'd just left as they were getting set upon by a swarm of Indians. Those savages were mostly on horseback, but a few were on foot too, and they were pouring up out of a stand of trees thick alongside the trail. Those braves were whooping and yelping and laying into whoever came to hand. Men, women, children, grannies. They didn't discriminate.

Going to the aid of those wagon train folks was the decent thing to do, but you couldn't blame us for pausing there on the trail to work a few calculations, to try to establish what the odds were of us surviving that good turn. Not that low odds would have held us back, but they were something we had to consider, all of us anyway except for Pawnee boy who knew dog soldiers when he saw them, and his grudge against their sort kept him from doing much thinking at all. He went tearing up the trail whooping and yipping with just his knife in hand.

"If those Indians don't kill him," is what I said, "the white folks surely will." That seemed clear, given the general savagery and upset, so what could we do but catch up to him and keep on going into the fight?

I had my Colt. Orla had the rifle, and Ira and Arturo were each armed with one of LJ Burke's smokewagons, but all that firepower wasn't much use where we were, because even if we hit just Indians, the bullets would pass on through and lodge in a Hungarian or a County Downer, so at first there we just yipped and bellowed too.

Coming out with all that racket kind of goosed us up and made us bolder than we might have been. That's how it felt anyway, and so charging up that wagon road, I came to better appreciate why Indians shouted like they did. Even that pack of dog soldiers, those miserable dregs and rejects, appeared to be shaken up a little by the uproar of us coming along.

All we needed was to lay into those boys on a couple of

fronts at once, and once they'd backed off from the white
folks to gauge what was doing with us, we opened up on
them with every gun we had. It proved enough to help
them discover the wisdom of withdrawal.

They left their wounded and their dead behind. Indians
aren't sentimental sorts, and the ones fit to ride went off at
full gallop, screeching all the way. Our Pawnee boy fell on
one of the braves they'd left behind and went at him with
his knife. I hadn't ever thought an Indian might scalp an
Indian until right then when Pawnee boy helped himself
to an ambitious slab of skin and hair. He held it high and
did that Indian yodel like they do, which rattled me then
when I heard it and rattles me now when I think about it.

He was lucky nobody among the Irish and Hungarians
shot him given what they'd just endured, but instead they
were restrained and grateful that we'd come back to help
them, and we didn't tell them it was only because of a
child who was kind of a witch.

Belle came up along about then to draw my attention
to the shovel, and we buried Hungarians and bog jumpers
for the balance of the day.

We left the next morning with a gunny sack full of biscuits as a show of appreciation, and we were traveling with
a Pawnee boy who'd gotten blooded in. I wouldn't have
guessed there was terribly much savage to him until that
scalping because he was timid and scrawny and liked his
whiskey way too much.

We sent Orla and Belle into Cactus Flats to make in-
quiries about Little Dusty, to let people know they were
his sisters and had come to take him home. Nobody they

talked to owned up to being acquainted with the man, but somehow word got back to him anyway.

We'd set up camp a mile or so away from the trading post—that and a church and a couple of shacks was about all Cactus Flats was—and we waited there for a few days, us and Little Dusty's sisters, and he came around like we'd figured he might in a while.

He didn't have any sisters, or had just a dead one, but once people in Cactus Flats had described the females looking for him and how handsome and well fitted out and solvent they'd seemed, Little Dusty couldn't help but be curious and maybe a little hopeful that he could somehow score some cash out of the thing.

That's what I figured. Trash has a way of being drawn to most anything with the faint smell of profit, so out he came one afternoon, rode up to pay a call just like Orla had told us he probably would.

She grabbed the man up in a sisterly embrace.

"Here he is!" she shouted Belle's way. "I told you we'd find him."

And Little Dusty quizzed Orla on where they'd come from and who the rest of us were—an Indian, a colored, a Mexican, and a boy. I couldn't really blame him for being curious.

Then he remembered he didn't have a sister and so almost certainly didn't have two. That's when Orla went faint and girlish and needed her brother to hold her up, so Little Dusty stepped up to offer support, to wrap his arms around Orla, which left her free to relieve him of both his pistols at once.

He was quick to figure out the brand of trouble he'd
walked into.

"Aw, hell," was the first thing he told us while he had
another look at an Indian, a colored, a Mexican, and a boy
but this time with fresh eyes. Then he turned his attention
to Orla who had his pistols pointed at him and took occasion to study Belle before speaking poorly of her dog.

"I ought to have stayed away from y'all," was the next
thing that he said before he assured us he hadn't done a
thing to the woman or the goat.

Then he sought permission to show us his flyer and
pulled it out of his pocket. It was worn at the creases and
torn here and there, and the likeness wasn't awfully true,
but the details were just about what we'd heard. The cash
payout, though, seemed low.

"Why only thirty dollars?" Ira was the one who asked
him that. Out of all of us, he'd turned out to be the one
with the head for numbers and was most pleased when
stuff all toted up.

That made Little Dusty's flyer a bit of a problem for Ira
since Little Dusty, in the details, was said to have killed
two humans and a goat that somebody somewhere had
thought just made him a thirty dollar outlaw. Even in our
limited experience, we'd seen less ambitious rascals go for
more.

Little Dusty, of course, reminded us that he'd only killed
the man and that was kind of an accident if you took time
to think about it. He claimed to half helped the fellow
tumble down some stairs.

"Hung on, the way I heard it," he said. "I was in Oklahoma by then."

"And the woman and the goat?" Ira asked him.

Little Dusty shot Orla chiefly a pleading look that I took to mean he thought, even in his diminished state, he was still above answering questions from an octoroon. Orla seemed to take that look the same exact way herself and responded by drawing both pistol hammers back.

"Somebody must have come along and done for them once I was gone. Or maybe…maybe," Little Dusty said, "didn't nobody kill them at all."

"Then how'd they get on here?" I had Little Dusty's flyer and waved it at him.

"Cause I ain't got no luck," is what he told me.

That was kind of a trend with rascals out there. We'd all taken notice of it and had even discussed it a time or two. Those boys were awfully quick to feel sorry for themselves. Yeah, they'd murdered people and robbed them, but wasn't this life hard and didn't things run against them more often than not.

"A day and a half to Pueblo from here?" Ira was doing his calculations.

I nodded like I had some idea where on this earth we were.

"Thirty dollars," Ira said, chiefly to Orla who had a mind for numbers too, and the rest of us were content to let that pair work out if it was worth the trip at all. Either we took Little Dusty in to the marshal or we cut him loose in hopes he'd become more valuable in time.

Little Dusty himself introduced a wrinkle when he offered us thirty-two dollars to turn him loose. He said that was all the money he had, but once we'd dug around, it turned out Little Dusty had forty-six dollars, with part of that in his underpants and the rest of it in a boot. So suddenly he was worth seventy-six dollars, and Ira announced he was happy with that.

Little Dusty, for his part, grew even more pitiful since that day had seen him both caught and robbed at a place he'd ridden out to even while knowing his sister was already dead.

"Ain't this how it goes." He sounded like he might cry, and I was so disappointed in him I wanted to smack him or spit, and I was trying to settle on one or the other when more company rode up on us.

Three men who, quite plainly, were trouble, and we all had reason to know who one of them was. He'd made a poor choice as far as hats go, and I guess he liked the look of it on him or somebody had told him it was sharp, but it wasn't sharp, and he came off underneath it like a fool.

He had to be Dupree. The hat was certainly a clue, but then we soon enough got a good look at his fancy saddle with all kinds of designs in the leather and lots of silver bits and bobs. It was the sort of saddle you'd ride on in a Mexico City parade, which played against and contradicted the hat.

So you could say Dupree was singular by way of a first impression, but it soon enough turned out he was just a lug with two sidekicks and a gun. A shotgun in Dupree's case with the barrels sawed off and walnut stock cut down too.

"Hey here," he told as he rode up. Dupree looked clean

but whiskery while the pair flanking him might have spent
the morning rolling around in the dirt. They had on regular hats that appeared to be stiffened and held together
by sweat, each stained with probably enough salt to cure a
heifer.

Dupree's was an authentic beaver top hat, but it looked
like maybe it had been made for a child. We'd been
warned it was too small for him, but that didn't quite say
enough because it would have been too small for him
when he was ten. The brim of it was tangled up in his
hair, and that appeared to be what was holding the thing
in place. It had a bullet hole in it two thirds of the way up
and a feather sticking out of the top.

"I'm gone be needing him," he told us and pointed at
Little Dusty with his nose. Then he spat again, and his
sidekicks spat. That appeared to be what they shared by
way of a hobby.

"For what?" Orla asked him.

Dupree pulled a folded handbill out of his shirtpocket
and proceeded to shake it until it opened up. He had the
same one Little Dusty was carrying.

"Got a price on him," Dupree told us. "Don't you,
boy?"

Little Dusty nodded and started in on how he hadn't
done a thing in this world to the woman or the goat.

"They'll sort it for you," Dupree told him, and then
all three of them spat again. "Come on," he said to Little
Dusty, which brought that business to a head.

One of us could have spoken up to tell Dupree we'd
landed Little Dusty first, so if anybody was going to take

him in for the reward, it seemed plain it was going to be us. Squabbling was almost certain to follow in advance of, most likely, gunplay. That meant people would get hurt or maybe killed over thirty dollars.

We didn't know what Dupree had loaded his shotgun with, and a stubby sawed-off like the one he was carrying across his fancy saddle is just the sort of weapon to make you remember you'd rather not get shot.

So once he'd said, "Come on," to Little Dusty, we all just stood there and thought about it.

Even Little Dusty appeared of two minds over what he ought to do. We'd been decent enough with him as far as it went, and you had to wonder about Dupree and his buddies. They didn't look the type to take much care with fellows they picked up.

So everything stopped for half a minute while we all looked at each other, and it was Ira who'd done the math on the thing and figured it all out. We had Little Dusty's pocket money, which was more than his reward, and we didn't much want to make the trip to Pueblo anyway since we preferred to stay out in the countryside where most of the rascals were.

That was his thinking, he'd tell us later, but as we were standing there looking around, all Ira did was shake his head like he was quitting on an auction. We knew what he meant, and so me and Orla together said to Little Dusty, "Go on."

Dupree and his buddies had seen what went on, and they found it good for a chuckle. Then they spat again, and Dupree winked and told us, "Nigger boss," while one of his sidekicks tied Little Dusty at the wrists and shoved him up onto his horse.

Ira, for his part, kept us calm by shaking his head again.

The three of them spat another time and went back the way they'd come. One of them had Little Dusty's reins in hand. They were maybe a quarter hour gone before we heard the gunshot. It seemed likely those boys had decided they'd rather have charge of a corpse since Little Dusty would have been hung anyway.

"For a scoundrel," I confessed, "I didn't mind him much."

I just hoped they hadn't shot him for the woman and the goat.

3

We dipped south to the Arkansas River and fooled around there a little while before making a push up north on the wagon road as far as Alma. That town was a haven for scallywags. One of their own had taken ownership of the saloon and the hotel. That's the story we heard anyway. Talk was he'd won them in a card game down around Texarkana where the brother of the actual owner had offered them up once his stake ran dry. When the fellow came to claim his winnings, him and the actual owner quarreled, which went the usual course from salty accusation to warm lead.

We thought about taking a couple of rooms in the Alma hotel, just to give us a break from sleeping rough with the mesa rats and the snakes, but they wouldn't let Ira past the lobby, so we reconsidered and camped out by a creek just west of town.

They had no problem at all in Alma with octoroons in their saloon, though they balked at first when our Pawnee boy came in too, but we'd done what we could to make him look like one of those broken red men. We'd put him in dungarees and a shirt after Orla had soaped him up and scrubbed him down in the creek. So the barkeep grumbled but served him, and our Pawnee was such an accomplished drinker that he won the respect of most everybody around him in due time.

I was just hoping he didn't get so whiskied up he'd want to wrestle because that was sure to end for him in gunplay or a knifing, so I tried to stay close to him and curb him when I could.

Orla proved to be a big hit in Alma's saloon because she was pretty and fair and wasn't selling herself for sex like the rest of the women in the place. They were rough and fragrant, those gals. They stank of eau de cowpoke and tried to cover more with face powder than face powder could hope to do. Orla, though, was unimproved because she didn't need it, and she was wearing trousers tight enough to show her shape along with a man's shirt she liked to leave about half unbuttoned, so you didn't need to be the least bit sly to see her underthings.

She carried Burke's derringer in her pocket, which left her prepared for two rounds of trouble. That seemed undergunned given how hotheaded Arturo was. He didn't care for the way men ogled her and bought her all the sherry she wanted, but I just kept reminding him that

Orla would find out stuff we needed to know and pro-
posed that she was safe out in the open in the saloon. That
even held until a fellow deep in his cups came stumbling
over to paw her.

At first, he offered her twenty dollars to take off her
pants, but when she gave him that laugh of hers that was
like shaking busted crystal, he decided he'd just reach out
and feel whatever he wanted for free.

Me and Arturo both were about to lay into the man
when Orla's assorted admirers beat us to it. They knocked
him to the floor and kicked him around for a while as they
simultaneously apologized to Orla and replaced the sherry
she'd spilled.

Those boys all seemed to enjoy being gentlemanly for
a change. Usually they yelled and swore and drank and
sometimes paid a woman for affection, so getting to scrape
and bow and have a civil exchange with a lady must have
felt like climbing off a horse after riding fifty miles. The
pleasure was all in the difference.

So we kept an eye on her but left Orla to herself and
turned our attention instead to all the abuse that Ira was
taking since our Pawnee had won the respect of the barkeep and his fellow patrons by drinking about twice as
much as them.

Of course, it was the trashiest men in there who felt
the need to bark at Ira because they could only get by
believing there were worse folks than themselves. If they
couldn't look down on an octoroon or a coolie or a gypsy,
then they'd be obliged to function as the lowest creatures
around.

So the polite ones called him *boy* while the other ones called him everything else, and there were maybe six or eight of them altogether. Ira had practice at ignoring their kind, and being Mexican, Arturo had long gotten plenty of guff as well, but I wasn't at all in the habit of suffering much jawboning from trash.

Back home in the mountains, we had lowlives by the bushel, but nobody around who was halfway decent took any mess off of them. You couldn't because they'd just crowd in and make you twice as sorry you hadn't caused them to suffer the first moment they popped off. In my experience, trashy people don't learn anything, so there's no point in waiting to bust them up, no point in trying to persuade them, in making a bid to bring them around to right and proper behavior. Being trash is as permanent as being an octoroon.

So I let the first two say snide things to Ira, but I happened to be in easy reach of the next boy who came along. He was ragged and nasty and looked, from his teeth, like he'd been chewing on a tree stump. He sidled up to Ira to explain exactly why he'd never let black folk into any business he might run. He had a list of reasons that started out with Ira's sort being animals and thieves and no smarter than most possums, and he seemed to be building to worse than that when I smacked him across the face.

"It's all right," Ira told me. He said he'd developed a hide.

I think I said back, "Naw," or something and waited on that trashy guy to get over his shock and come straight at me so I could hit him a time or twelve again.

I'd smacked him with my open hand because that was sure to win his attention while providing me a gap to warn him that I'd soon be making a fist.

Being trash, he was a coward and so needed reinforcements, but his buddies hadn't done anything to get beat up about.

To discourage them further, I went ahead and punched their pal in the face, and once he made a swing my way and missed, I hit him two times more. Then a second trashy guy came charging at me. He had a knife out—rusty, of course, and too small for the job—so I stepped back to let him jab it and then closed in to flatten his nose. He dropped on top of the first boy who'd stayed down on the saloon plank floor.

Even though I never threw another punch, I did get blamed for the general mayhem. Seeing me fight had reminded the patrons of grudges they were holding and punches they had long been meaning to throw, so soon enough most everybody in the Alma saloon was brawling and busting up whatever of the decor came to hand. Me and Ira and Arturo stayed where we were and watched the goings on. Orla was over across the way with Belle, but she had three or four protectors who stood abreast to make sure none of the brawlers bounced their way.

A couple of lawmen showed up in a while. They turned out to be part time deputies who worked for the Alma sheriff. He was kind of an enterpriser and seemed to have business interests around. I found all that out because I was the one who got arrested. Both of those deputies fired into the ceiling to quiet the patrons down and then asked who'd kicked that business off. Most everybody agreed it had been me.

They had a lone cell in Alma and put me in it.

"He'll be back midday maybe," is what one of the deputies told me.

"Who?" I asked him.

"Ruben."

That didn't help a lot, and I must have looked it.

"He's the sheriff," the talking deputy said. The other was fooling with the buttons on his shirt. "Owns the saloon and the hotel too."

And that's how I got the story of the way he'd won them playing cards, or had won them in part and then came to Alma where he finished the acquisition.

"I guess I could pay for some damage," I said. I had a sense that's where things were going.

"Yeah," the talking deputy told me. "I guess you could."

They wouldn't allow visitors for me until Orla and Belle came by, a shapely woman in pants and a child they couldn't know was a witch. The deputies gave those two twenty minutes to see me, let them right into the cell where Orla told me my bunch would bust me out if I wanted.

"I think it's all about money," is what I said. "How tore up is the place?"

She shrugged. Orla might have been classy, but she was also Irish and so had seen too many drunk men bust up stuff before to think a fight in a saloon was any big deal.

"A few chairs. Some tables. Bottles and stuff," she said.

"They've got to wait on the sheriff," I was telling her just as the sheriff himself walked in.

He had saddlebags over his shoulder and a rifle in his hand but didn't look dusty and horse-worn like most of the men around. That turned out to be because he took a wagon everywhere, was a kind of a commuting sort who made gentle trips place to place.

It was easy to see how he'd gotten ahead in both the saloon and the sheriff business. He was one of those men who looked like the Lord had made him with His own hands. His jaw was square, and his nose was straight, and his eyes were a blue that caught your notice. He was big at the shoulders and slight at the waist, and once he'd lifted his hat, his hair didn't look like it had suffered from it at all.

If I'd had a hotel and a saloon, I'd have been tempted to give them to him because he impressed me as one of those fellows whose way in the world was bound to work out.

And it wasn't just me. Orla saw it all too. She subjected that sheriff to the brand of study I'd yet to see her inflict on a man, and when she told him her name, she offered him her fingers as well. He knew to take them while making a short, sharp bow like I'd figured he probably would.

"R.W. Walls," he told her. "But most folks call me Ruben." Then he did that thing where he reached towards Belle and pulled a nickel out of her ear. She failed to giggle, like maybe he'd hoped, but only tooted instead.

"Bring him on out," the sheriff instructed one of his deputies, pointing at me and then asked the other one, "How'd this all get kicked off?"

"It was Luther and them," that deputy said. "Colored

boy set them off."

"So where's he?"

"He didn't do nothing," the deputy who was unlocking my cell door told him. "It was this one here that went on and put Luther down."

"That so?" the sheriff asked me.

I nodded. "He didn't think my friend was fit to be inside. I disagreed."

Just then, Sheriff Ruben noticed the list of damages the barkeep had put together, plucked it off the desk he'd perched on and eyeballed it up and down.

"Looks like you had some help with the disagreeing," is what the sheriff told me.

"Lively bunch in there," Orla told him. "He just punched the one."

I'd only ever seen her look like that at Arturo on occasion, and if I was honest that was all the way back when they were living with the Cheyennes.

"Well," Sheriff Ruben said, "y'all got about twelve dollars?"

Orla nodded. She smiled. "We'll have Ira bring it."

I asked that bunch, "Y'all let colored boys in here?" That was what I had instead of a sneery look.

Those deputies weren't so sure if they did, but Sheriff Ruben knew what I was after, and he grinned and winked. Even his teeth were perfect too.

Orla offered to stay back as collateral and send me and Belle after the money. The sheriff told her that wasn't necessary as he was pulling out a chair so Orla could park herself and hang around.

I told Belle on the way back to camp that Orla was clearly smitten. I even owned up to being slightly smitten myself.

"You get anything off of him?" I asked her. "Anything worth tooting about?"

She didn't care for it when I talked to her like she was a fur-bearing divining rod who could turn on being witchy and then switch it off again.

"Arturo won't like it." By then I was talking more to myself than her. "Hate to see something like this get us all messed up."

I was still at that age when I thought of a woman as a complication. You'd be going along feeling nothing much and getting your business done. Maybe you loved your horse or your mule, had some boots shaped to your feet, and kept your pistol lubricated so it never let you down. That all came across as satisfying and functioned well enough, and you told yourself you didn't need a woman to undo it, to say your mount was a nag, your boots weren't fit for company, and you had to leave your rifle and your buntline in the barn because a house was for china and boudoir chairs and rugs on all the floors.

Of course, I didn't have any personal experience with women beyond the grappling I'd gotten up to with some girls, but that hadn't kept me from making an uninformed determination that romancing a woman was like a prickly thicket you had to fight your way through.

Back at camp, Arturo (naturally) only wanted to hear about Orla and what had possessed us to leave her on her own in that town full of low men.

I attempted to give him a picture of RW Walls that made him sound less than ideal and tried to do it by not describing him at all. I made him out to be a man in a hat with a badge who wanted twelve dollars from us when, by rights, he could have asked us for a whole hell of a lot more.

That was good enough for Ira. He kept the money bag due to his head for numbers and the fact that we were all perfectly satisfied trusting an octoroon.

My problem, at bottom, was that I didn't have much of a grip on how women worked. Or women anyway in the person of Orla who'd thrown over her brand new husband on their honeymoon to take up with a Mexican gentleman she'd only known for a day and a half. So even I could make the case that Orla was the sort of creature to act on a first impression, and Arturo certainly knew that from being on Ruben's end of things. So he took charge of our twelve dollars, saddled his horse, and set out towards Alma at something north of a trot.

We watched him go, me and Ira, Belle and our Pawnee boy, and since I was the only one who'd been in the jailhouse and could talk about it, I said, "That sheriff's so pretty I'd kiss him on the mouth."

"He won't go kill him, will he?" Ira wanted to know. Arturo was little more than a speck up the way and a plume of dust by then.

"Doubt it," I said, "though he's almost sure to unload some poetry on him."

"Maybe we ought to go," he suggested.

Belle tooted. The Pawnee boy grunted. That was enough

for me, so we all went.

Arturo and Sheriff Ruben were having what looked like a conversation out in front of the jail house while Orla stood by and tossed in the odd, "Now, boys." It seemed only to have the effect of egging them on.

I could see, as we approached, the sheriff had our money in hand, so I figured all we needed to do was draw Arturo and Orla clear and let them work out whatever they needed to off and alone in the countryside.

I caught the sheriff's eye as we reached the jailhouse. "We good?" is what I asked him.

He showed me the scrip in his fist and then suffered a couplet from Arturo. That man knew more poetry in Spanish and English than should have been allowed by law. He could almost always dredge up verse that was at least marginally pertinent, and he was happy to unload it on you and then tell you what it meant.

I was on Gunther who wouldn't have stood to be left alone in camp with no people to bite and no horses to kick to pieces, so I'd ridden him in, and he was braying and chuffing loud and long enough to all but drown Arturo out.

That would have been a good thing with most folks spouting poetry, but Arturo was cursed with dogged determination, so he just waited for Gunther to settle down and started all over again. Arturo set in with Spanish and then came out with his own poetical translation. It was something about a serpent that had slipped into a convent and was making a problem for several of the nuns.

I couldn't imagine there'd be much benefit for us from

hearing what it meant, so I spoke up and asked Arturo if maybe we shouldn't be moving along.

"Thank you, sheriff," I said. "Appreciate your understanding."

"It is a snake, you see, in with the women." There was no making Arturo quit.

"Don't want that," Ruben told him, but not in a personal, pointed way. He seemed more like a man making an earnest effort to tolerate poetry with some grace.

Then I'll be damned if Arturo didn't dredge up an additional scrap of verse, something about a crocodile lurking in a pond. I imagine by then even Pawnee boy was getting the thrust of the thing. Orla surely was and made kind of a Gunther noise Arturo's way before coming away from the jailhouse to mount double up with Belle. She took the reins and whipped Belle's bay around and off the two of them went.

That let the air out of Arturo but only after one couplet further that he didn't even bother to translate before he mounted up and left.

Me and Ira and Pawnee boy watched him go along with Sheriff Ruben.

"Odd one, your Mexican," the sheriff said.

"Loves her to bits," is what I told him, which was a thing I used to hear sometimes about my folks back home, but usually only after one of their dust ups. Often, Daddy would have gone at her, but sometimes Momma had had enough of him to swat him with a stick of wood or kick him in his dangles. Then somebody—a neighbor or cousin usually—would feel the need to tell us that, evidence aside, they loved each other to bits.

And there I was saying the same damn thing to a Sheriff in Colorado in a bid to paper over the Orla and Arturo cracks I'd seen. They'd still snuggle up plenty, and sometimes they'd retire with a blanket off and alone, but I'd been getting a sense, especially from Orla, that their thing was wearing thin.

Arturo was a tireless romantic with all grades of fanciful ideas about the course love ought to take and the flavor it should have for two people who've found their match and joined up in a kind of bond. He never quite seemed willing to factor in erosion and the wear that comes with rubbing up against the same people every day. Even lovely Irish lasses who've cast their husbands aside and rangy, handsome Mexicans who might be wellsprings of verse.

My fear was Orla would take up with Sheriff Ruben before she'd allowed Arturo the time he'd need to grieve. I imagined her staying on in the town of Alma and Arturo heading back across the Rio Grande, which would leave just me and Pawnee boy, along with Ira and Belle, and we hardly impressed as anything like a formidable quartet. I wondered if maybe I should resign myself to going on to California so as to pan enough to purchase passage on a ship around Cape Horn in hopes of finding my way to the Chesapeake and back east.

I'd let Belle come if she wanted. I'd gotten as far as settling on that and guessed I'd work out how to counsel Ira and situate Pawnee boy. This was all on account of the feeling I'd drawn from Orla in the jailhouse the moment that sheriff with the square jaw and blue eyes walked in.

"Is there a Mrs. Ruben?" I asked the sheriff. That seemed like a thing worth knowing.

He pinched his lips together, and his blue eyes went all glisteny. He had a glance at the sky and one down the road before he told me, "There is." Then he explained that she was suffering from some kind of nervous condition and was hardly anymore the woman he'd brought out from Wichita.

I offered my sympathies but was secretly pleased the sheriff had a wife.

Once we'd reached camp, I found Orla and Arturo in the throes of one of their quarrels, what they called spirited give and takes. Ordinarily, I would have given them as wide a birth as I could manage, but in this instance I thought it best to walk up and let them know how I'd left it with the sheriff.

Then I made like it was an afterthought when I said, "His wife's kind of sick." I hoped that would serve as a sort of punctuation.

But then Orla asked, "How sick exactly?" and those two started in again.

rturo made sure we packed up camp and got away from the town of Alma, but Orla made just as certain that we didn't go too far. She got quite a lot more interested in who we could round up where. It seemed clear to me she had designs on taking some scoundrels to Ruben since he was handier, and far more comely, than the marshal down in Pueblo. She never said as much but displayed a brand of interest in our flyers that she'd never come close to showing off before.

Arturo, for his part, made for a while like everything was fine, and he'd unfreight on us scraps of verse where love was holding and passion was steady. He seemed to want to believe if a poet had written it down, it was probably true. While the rest of us hadn't yet talked it over, we all seemed to know trouble was brewing and so didn't make the usual exasperated noises whenever Arturo trotted some doggerel out.

Then, of course (like is ordinarily the case), the not talking about it became its own problem, and we were all spending way too much effort remembering what to not mention and dodge. That meant most everything we did talk about arose from calculation, which had a way of snuffing out the spark and fun.

They still slept under a blanket together, and Orla still permitted Arturo to kiss her every morning once he'd aired some piece of verse devoted to the beauty and wonder of dawn. But nothing was right exactly, and there wasn't a one of us who didn't feel it. Even our homely dog was anxious, and Gunther certainly knew what was up. He had uncanny powers of discernment for a mule.

Finally, Belle was the one to speak up. She watched Arturo and Orla of a morning go through what had gotten to be for them a dumbshow of romance, and then she tooted twice and snorted once. I knew precisely what she meant. The girl was warning that change would be with us soon and nothing would be like it was.

So we had upset and problems on the horizon but were still at the stage where we were pretending everything was fine. That involved a lot of choosing to talk about hardly anything and instead, around our fire at night, suffering Pawnee boy to sing. That fellow loved to warble, but in ordinary times we were quick to shut him down. He couldn't hit a note, usually failed to even crowd one, but would carry on in the Indian style and raise a grunting, tuneless mess.

So that's what we had for a couple of weeks, and I like to think I came, through Pawnee boy, to appreciate Indian singing. Hearing him grunt and chant and chuff for an appreciable stretch some nights allowed me to settle into the lovely melancholy of it. The Indian rhythm and Indian tones and the march of them over time hinted at a sadness far larger and longer than most of us will ever know.

I'm sure Pawnees around wouldn't have picked him as their best tribal example, but he was fierce on the traditions in his way. He could read a track all right and predict the weather if you listened to him, and he was bold in a fight, was a terror with a knife or even just a stick of wood. When he was singing, he was the true Indian his elders would have wished him to be.

So that was a benefit of our circumstances. Pawnee boy came into his own. Another virtue was our renewed sense of focus. We'd been making a jab at finding outlaws we could cash in, but we'd gotten to where we weren't steady about it, partly due to the danger involved and partly to the travel in and out of Pueblo City, and maybe partly to the killing we'd likely have to get up to for convenience's sake. The farther you needed to haul a man known for his lawless behavior, the more the temptation to render him a lifeless sack of meat.

Often, they'd give you cause to do it. Those fellows didn't get on handbills due to an appetite for surrender, and they all preferred a bullet to a noose, so you had to be cagey and lucky to tie up a live one and take him in, which called for more effort than we could muster every

day and all the time. Too often we'd end up no better than
Dupree with his filthy sidekicks and his hat.

That wore on us, consequently, or it wore on me anyway because I was only sixteen years old (at least that's
what they tell me) and maybe six months gone from the
first man I ever killed. Yes, he'd been a Comanche, and he
meant me harm, so he'd helped me along by being both
treacherous and deserving, but still he was a man I'd put
a bullet in, a man whose life I'd taken, and I'd somehow
thought it would be enough to harden up after him.

That Comanche, though, was an easy one, like chopping the head off a snake, but the rest had mostly been
white men in various states of depravity. It wasn't always so
clear a thing that those boys had it coming, which left it to
me and my conscience to compensate.

So we were better off probably plotting and planning
just as a way to keep us from talking about Sheriff Ruben
and his blue eyes. Or as a way to keep Arturo and Orla
from dwelling on the man since we had scoundrels and
rapscallions to inquire about and locate.

Me and Orla were the best at that. She could work her
way with men by being a pretty lass, and I could engage as
a lad on his own making a bid to be upstanding.

All I had to do was say "Yes sir" and "Yes ma'am" whenever somebody had left me the room.

So it got to where just us two would engage with the
frontier public. When I showed a handbill and asked after
some rascal, I'd usually say he'd killed my brother, had shot
him off of his horse when all we were doing was heading
to California to pan for a little gold. That would always

serve to grab them because a lot of them had brothers and so knew how they'd feel if what had happened to mine had happened to theirs.

We worked our way north, but Orla made sure we stayed within sensible striking distance of greater Alma town. That came to mean we'd usually turn around once we'd spied Quandary Peak, and Orla and Arturo would argue about that as a stand in for quarreling over Sheriff Ruben. Arturo would generally try to push us as far as Mt. Argentine, but Orla would only ever permit the man a quick dash up to Hoosier. Then we'd work our way back south toward Alma. She'd get happy. He'd go glum.

In terms of practical results, nothing changed very much, and that was largely because the territory was infested with lawless scum. Few of them ever claimed to not be the rascals their flyers held them to be, though they'd frequently take some issue with the listed exploits and charges. To boil it down, a lot of them hadn't killed the woman or the goat, but that still usually left them attached to a couple of corpses. We'd let a few of them slide, but we made it a policy to always take in that sort who'd clearly enjoyed it all too much.

They were thick on the ground, that kind. You hardly needed the week or two with them we'd required to sort out Ira. They'd always tell you or show you right away that something inside them had simply let go.

Almost all of them were from some city back east, and it didn't seem to matter if it was New York or Toledo. They'd been regular men (mostly) doing regular things, working ordinary work and living their lives in ordinary ways until they'd indulged an itch to check out the frontier before the frontier was gone. Like me, more than a few of them had killed an Indian or two and then discovered there wasn't much of a price to pay for having done it. The law didn't care, and any regrets they'd felt thinned out and went away because they'd only killed an Indian after all.

Once you've fired a bullet into a man, you're likely to repeat it if only because you've swamped that part of your soul that holds you back. I like to think we're all born knowing we shouldn't take another life, even before our daddies tell us or our preachers bring it home, but once you've killed, it's like you've pulled on a wishbone and busted it in half. There's no putting any of it back together.

That isn't to say it gets easier to kill a man, but it sure becomes more likely because you've already known whatever goes with killing men before, which isn't enough to stop you and gets to be less and less over time. After a while, too much pluck and willpower are required to keep some men from pulling a trigger, and if they weren't weak against urges anyway, they wouldn't be where they were.

That was pretty much my practice and philosophy out there. We'd identify a scoundrel and then give him a chance to let us believe his offense was a one-time thing. If he came off seeming contrite and not remotely proud of his charges, we'd negotiate a sum we'd take to let him have the road and leave.

That was our rule, and that was our practice, and we'd become scrupulous about it after we'd grabbed up a preacher and his wife. He went by Reverend Williford and held her out as Rachel. Then he uncorked a load of palaver about her namesake in the Bible who'd married her cousin, traveled the wilderness, and birthed the tribes of Israel. The man needed close to a quarter hour just to cover that.

We'd stopped on the wagon road to chat those two up because we were carrying a handbill that featured a man and a woman sort of like them. Not a preacher and his wife but a fellow from St. Louis who was traveling with a cousin posing as his personal secretary. They were thought to have strangled to death a couple of widow ladies. One in the Kansas territory and another back in Texas. They both ran boarding houses and had taken these two in.

The motive was given out as robbery, though they hadn't made off with much and had gone to inordinate trouble tying those widows to their beds. They'd also left them gussied up in finery. Frilly dresses, Easter bonnets, cheek rouge like a clown would wear. In the cities back east, that sort of thing would have earned them a reputation for being off the beam a little and odd, but out where we were, they were just two more faces on a flyer who, if you brought in the pair, were good for eighty dollars. They weren't said to be dangerous unless you were a widow with a good dress and a bed.

The two we met came off at first as what they said they were. The man we knew as Reverend Williford was dull enough to be a preacher, and his Rachel was sufficiently mousy and obedient to seem a preacher's wife. They impressed me as a bit peculiar, but I laid that off to them being Presbyterian. I'd never met one before and was prepared to make allowances for that.

Orla, though, noticed that the preacher appeared to have painted his lips and dusted his eyelids. I knew he looked off center, but I let Presbyterian cover that too until the Reverend Williford took an unnatural interest in what he called Orla's decolletage, and he informed her she'd be sight to behold in probably thirty years.

If you give people enough time, they'll usually end up being precisely who they are. Even a man as well practiced as the reverend couldn't keep his proclivities at bay, and that was after we'd told him we were out on the wagon road hunting scoundrels. So he had to be aware of what he was potentially giving up—the freedom to stop at the next boarding house and strangle the next widow woman and steal just enough stuff to keep most folks from thinking he was merely a decolletage man.

Just after he'd told Orla how lovely her cleavage would come to be, she leveled the rifle at him and said, "All right. I guess that'll do."

He turned out to be wearing a whalebone corset and a piece of hosiery, and his Rachel proved to be a woman he'd come across in Topeka. She was the one who told us everything they'd been up to, which included a pile of dead ladies who hadn't been blamed on those two yet.

The reverend never tried to cut her off but just stood there in his women's wear correcting the odd detail.

The more they talked, the jollier Orla got because she knew she'd soon be seeing handsome Sheriff Ruben. Arturo, of course, went the other way from knowing she'd be seeing him too.

We were three days from Alma when we took charge

of that pair and so were obliged to endure their company long enough to grow unsettled. The reverend was conspicuously bent and peculiar, but his partner was the one of them who troubled me more. She was ordinary in a lot of ways but with gaps that made her treacherous, or left her indifferent anyhow to what was right and wrong. She didn't like untidy people, thought grubbiness a moral failing, and she said that was why she took against Pawnee boy.

"Can't help it," she told us and shook her head. "I'd kill him if you'd let me."

She'd personally strangled, we came to find out, about half the folks they'd killed. Most of them women in a weakened, elderly state, but she'd done in a couple of Cherokee grandpas who'd been too drunk to stop her, and the reverend allowed his Rachel had ended the life of a child as well.

"Tragic," he told us and explained she'd done it out of irritation. Then he assured us all that the meek, in fact, would not likely inherit this earth.

Shortly thereafter, that woman displayed a kind of interest in Belle. By then, we were keeping them tied up all the time since it seemed clear they couldn't be trusted. She claimed to have soaked in the flavor of Belle just from riding beside her, and it got to where she'd say, "I see you, sugar," three or four times a day.

There near the end, when we were almost to Alma, that lady picked me out specifically and called me over to her. "That child," she said of Belle on her bay, "is a fairy of the air." Then she winked and showed me the tip of her tongue. "But you know that already."

I don't think I managed to say much of anything back, but I remember hoping that Sheriff Ruben and his crew would hang those two and quick. They seemed less like criminals than a blight on decency. There was something black at the core of the both of them, most especially her. At first, I thought she was doing whatever her preacher/partner wanted and had probably indulged the man because she was weak. But in the course of three days, I came to see that she was the dastardly one and he only had the occasional taste for violence against ladies, especially if she'd see to it and he could watch.

The longer I was around them, the worse I felt. I think that was true for all of us except our homely dog. He didn't care who spilled out on the ground the beans they couldn't eat.

By the time we reached Alma, we had chapter and verse on everything they'd done, and they felt far different from all the other rascals we'd brought in. Those boys were bold and greedy, for the most part, and weak against the pull of whiskey while that preacher and his lady friend were bent and savage without a tipple at all.

Worse still, they were proud of themselves and convinced they were only showing us what was coming.

"In the last days," that preacher told us more than once, "some shall depart from the faith, giving heed to seducing spirits and doctrines of demons."

I remember him finding me once with a glance while he was talking about end times and all that. He gave me what I took to be a morsel of advice. "Devil up, son," is what he said.

Him with his red lips, his powdered eyelids, and his ladies' underthings. He was the man I'd see clear to take my
counsel from. That weighs on me still. Seducing spirits.
Doctrines, he told us, of demons. I guess when you're hard
against it, the devil sometimes is your friend.

Sheriff Ruben and his deputies took those two for what
they looked like—a preacher with more color to his com-
plexion than maybe the wind and sun had managed and
his prim lady associate who probably should have stayed
safe in some town back east.

We showed him the handbill, took our money, and
left it to Orla to tell Sheriff Ruben and his deputies too,
"They're vile."

Then we all came away from Ruben's jailhouse like our
stuff was done and we'd be leaving. Orla, though, raised a
noise I recognized as the worst thing Arturo could hear. It
was something from her neck that made it clear she wasn't
quite ready to leave.

Arturo was in a different place by then. I got the sense
that Orla had been bringing him around to her being finished with him, and not because he was a disappointment
or made problems with his poetry but more on account of
how she was the sort of woman who simply went through
men. It was only bad news for Arturo if you failed to consider that Orla was destined to run through Sheriff Ruben
after a while, and then maybe Arturo could show back up
and have a turn again. When I tried to sell him on that
way of thinking, I just got doggerel back.

So Orla made a noise in her neck and then returned

to the jailhouse. She stayed for twenty minutes while we waited in the road.

"He's got a wife," I reminded Arturo in a bid to be consoling.

That prompted a couplet from Arturo on the wages of faithlessness. That's what he told us anyway because that business was in French.

Then things grew rowdy once Gunther had sunk his teeth in the haunch of the horse I was riding. She bucked, of course, and got all the other horses stirred up too. That was kind of the point, I had to think. Gunther enjoyed a melee, and as a bonus Belle just then had one of her fits. She warbled and snorted and tooted a bit as a kind of warning and preamble in advance of Dupree and his bunch riding toward us up the road.

He'd added another associate as grubby as the other two, and they'd collected what looked like four corpses draped across a couple of ponies.

Once Dupree had reached us, he spat and told us, "Y'all."

"Who you got?" Ira asked them, but they all ignored him because he was an octoroon.

"Isn't the Goins brothers, is it?" I eventually said.

Dupree lifted his tiny top hat to scratch his head before he shook it and spat some more. "Missed them by a day up at Clancy. Them boys having a time."

Dupree had a glance at the bodies they'd hauled, all four of them wrapped in blankets and bound up tight. "Mark them off," he said and pulled out two handbills, one of them for three boys who'd robbed a train and another for a fellow who'd knifed a cousin of his to death over a pig.

I reciprocated with the flyer for our preacher and his lady friend.

"Eighty for these two?" Dupree seemed to think them over-valued.

"Killed a pile of women." That was Arturo talking, but Dupree and his boys were far too fine to engage with a Mexican.

The new associate in particular appeared to object to Arturo and offered up a curdled look before he dredged some phlegm and spat.

Along about then, Orla stepped out of the jailhouse with Sheriff Ruben, and they took leave of each other like two people who'd rather not. Then Orla came our way. She had to pass Dupree and his bunch to reach us. The two old hands just gawked. Dupree raised his puny top hat, but the new guy eyed Orla's decolletage and said generally, "Well, shit."

That earned him a scrap of poetry. This bit sounded to be in Latin. Then Arturo pulled out his pistol and shot that fellow once.

5

It was a good thing he wasn't using one of the smokewagons we'd confiscated but had instead brought out the derringer and only hit the man in the arm. It's a wonder that bullet even got through his filthy sleeve and grit, but somehow it punctured the skin, and he bled a little. It wasn't enough of a wound to rate a response, which was why we all drew on the man. That included Dupree and the other two who didn't want him gunning for Arturo since we'd all probably shoot each other to bits right there in the road. That was the way back then out there. Stuff got out of hand in a hurry.

"Easy now," Sheriff Ruben told us all and waded in among us with his blue eyes, his square chin, his white teeth, and his stubble. Nobody wanted a bullet in him because he was too damn pretty to die.

Orla might have been making her swooning noises if she'd not been fixed on Arturo. He got one of those piercing lady looks meant to convey how very disappointed she was that Arturo hadn't sat quietly out in the road and not shot a man.

He felt bad about it, naturally. Being a romantic, Arturo knew he was only behaving like wounded lovers sometimes do, lashing out from a blend of impulse and heart-sick grief. He didn't need to be wrestled off his horse and volunteered himself to Ruben once he'd apologized to Orla with no doggerel at all.

The shot guy couldn't, of course, leave it alone. At first he made like getting shot, for him, was nothing, and then he had himself a leisurely, lingering look Orla's way before he announced where exactly he'd like to bury his face.

Ruben helped him halfway there by jerking him down and letting him land on his shot arm instead of his feet. Dupree found that to be ill treatment for one of his crew and said as much to Sheriff Ruben who told him, "Well," or something like it. He might have been meaning to carry on further, but just then I saw the preacher and his lady friend slip out of the jailhouse and leave the general area at a trot.

"Look there," I told the Sheriff and directed his attention up the road.

"Aw, hell," he said. "Go get them."

Me and Ira and Pawnee boy kicked our mounts but not before I said to Sheriff Ruben, "We'll be wanting eighty again."

That was kind of a mistake, as it turned out, because

Dupree was wearing spurs and sank them, so off he went ahead of us all, and Dupree caught up with the good reverend and his personal secretary while they were fooling with a wagon they meant to steal.

He said something to them. They said something back, and then Dupree leveled his stumpy shotgun, fired twice, and left them dead.

It was awful to see, and most of the great and good of Alma township saw it because they were out in the main road on that sunny afternoon.

"Killed folks," Dupree announced to them all by way of justification, and when the wagon's owner came out of the Alma bank to find a pair of chewed-up corpses on his buckboard, Dupree helpfully told him a few buckets of water would sluice the blood away.

"That's no way to do," Ira declared to anybody who cared to hear it. We were all in agreement with him but for the fellow Arturo had shot who told us how little he needed to know the opinion of a nigger, which earned the man a healthy few kicks from the Sheriff and Orla both. Arturo joined in as well, though he was a little late about it. He seemed bothered to see Orla and Ruben sharing something like a pastime.

The worst part was that Sheriff Ruben wanted us to give over our eighty that we'd spent three days earning while suffering exposure to that preacher and her. And Orla, because it was Ruben's, found it a capital idea.

"Only fair," she told us, or told Ira primarily since he'd be the one who'd have to count out the cash.

That's love in a nutshell, if you ask me—getting up to

dumb stuff for bad reasons. Then Dupree announced our eighty might help him forgive our Mexican for shooting his colleague over hardly anything.

So we gave him our money, and then I watched him ride right up to Belle and click at her as he chucked her under the chin. "Be good, sweet thing," Dupree said and set off down the road.

His two unshot boys followed while his shot one needed help up onto his horse but couldn't, somehow, find anybody willing, so he walked off with his reins in hand while muttering us all to perdition.

"You might want to check on your deputies," was a suggestion I had for Ruben.

It turned out the preacher had beat one of them senseless with a chair while his personal assistant had gone at the other with a fork. She'd left him comprehensively poked and perforated.

"Told you they were vile," Orla reminded the sheriff and then hurried us out of town to leave Ruben to dwell on her fair beauty and her wisdom. I guess she figured that would bring him around to hungering for her in time, and the way things went, I have to think it must have.

Nothing was the same for us after that. Orla and Arturo stopped sharing a blanket and would only sit on opposite sides of the fire. It's chore enough bringing in desperados when you're all rowing together, so it's prickly business when you've got open conflict in your bunch. Those times we'd talk to Arturo, Orla would blame us for taking his side, and if we chatted with Orla for even ten minutes, Arturo would go mopey. That was no way of living that can last for long.

I managed, at least, to get Orla to give Ira rifle lessons because it seemed clear to me she'd be shifting her decolletage into Alma soon, and she showed him how to aim and how best to lead his prey, but Ira didn't have the instinct for it that Orla clearly did. The racket of gunshots made him nervous, and he had no stomach for blood. Arturo, though, was staying too worked up to have charge of a rifle, and Pawnee boy only held guns by the barrels and whacked folks with the butts.

We'd been out of Alma only a week when we found some dead homesteaders and one live one among them who'd been half hacked to bits. We gave him water. He wasn't going to make it and wasn't after us to do anything but was content to have folks come and sit while he sank and faded.

He described who'd set upon them. They'd been whites and Indians both, a half dozen of them joined together for some spirited marauding. We showed him all the flyers we had, but nobody seemed to fit, and he'd had the impression a savage was in charge. He knew it sounded peculiar but said that was the feeling he got.

"One ear on him," he told us. He said his head was all scarred up like somebody had held him down in a fire. As for the rest of them, they were just fat and smelly. Smelly was normal out that way, but fat was kind of uncommon on account of what a chore it was to get anything decent to eat.

He died in a little while, so we got up to our customary business. Arturo sifted through the verse in his head and

came out with something fitting, after which Ira led us all
in a hymn, and Pawnee boy capped the service off with
a dance and a spot of chanting. Then we drew lots to see
who'd do the digging first.

I lost. I always seemed to lose, maybe because it was my
shovel.

We were a day and a half burying them all. Five grown
folks and one child, and they'd been living together in a
sapling shack that was hardly fit for chickens. I can't imagine why they seemed, even to savages, worth the bother of
killing. There was nothing to steal, and that bunch wasn't
doing a thing but scraping by.

"Who'd come through here," I asked out loud, "and
think this needed doing?"

"Let's find out." Ira pointed the way they'd left. We
could all see their tracks.

"No paper on them," Orla said.

She was right about that, as far as we knew, so if we
happened to catch and kill them, it'd be chiefly because
we felt offended by everything they'd done. That wasn't
business. That was vengeance with probably no place for
Ruben in it.

"Let's see what we see," I said to them all and rode off
where that crew had gone, just me on my pony pulling
Gunther behind us. I left it to everybody else to let me
lead them or not.

Ira came first with Belle and Arturo following close behind him along with our homely dog. Arturo even loosed
a couplet on the way, something about doing a righteous
thing no matter if you pay with your life. That was for

Orla, I had to think. Arturo wasn't much of a fighter, but Pawnee boy was, and he joined us once he'd turned his pony around.

That left Orla, and we were still close enough to Alma town to allow her to make the break with us she was clearly angling for. So I wouldn't have been surprised at all if she'd ridden off in the other direction.

Instead, she came our way while saying, "They'll probably kill us all."

So I got to be boss on a kind of fool's errand, which felt a bit worse than I'd hoped.

That bunch was easy to track because they killed everything they could. People. Buffalo. A goose. Four dogs and somebody's milk cow. We simply followed a trail of carcasses while wondering who in the world those fellows were.

We had an Indian with us, so it wasn't like whites and savages couldn't happen, but you had to figure that bunch would have earned some paper on them somewhere if we were in a world where a girl associate and a preacher in a corset could kill widows enough to rate a handbill of their own. These boys were slaughtering everything but didn't appear to be earning from it. Homesteaders and livestock had little to offer, so that crew just seemed bloodthirsty and out for a nasty thrill.

The way I figured it, a few of them probably had their reasons. They felt served poorly one way or another by something that had gone on and had let it fester and sour them on this world. The rest were wicked to start with and had come along for the chance to go wild.

We'd had a bunch back in the Alleghenies who'd gone
on a killing spree, and all of it had started with a man
whose wife fell off a ladder, some shiftless contraption
his brother-in-law had built. So he began by beating his
brother-in-law, but when that failed to satisfy him, he
went on a spree and lost his bearings entirely over time.
That made him a kind of magnet for people who already
had no bearings, and they all joined up and terrorized the
mountains for a bit.

They'd kill some of us. We'd kill some of them. There
was no chance that any of those boys were coming back to
regular life, so the army marched out from Richmond and
went to war on that whole pack. They made no attempt to
take them alive because nobody by then could see the use
in trying to lock them up. That happens sometimes when
people get wracked around and twisted. They go so far
that all you can do is drop them where they went.

That's what I expected with this mixed up crew, and I
told our bunch as much the first night we camped while
stalking. And I said expressly to Belle that the shovel
wasn't leaving Gunther's pack. She didn't even make a
noise or give me a salty look because we all of us understood that we were on a tidy up, and about a day and a
half later, that's precisely what it came to.

That bunch had shown up at a ranch near a place called
Silverheels, which was little more than a roadhouse, part
dry goods and part saloon. Two men in that roadhouse
were shot up along with a woman alive and about half
naked. She was the one who pointed us to the ranch where
those boys were having a bloody fit. They were killing

everything and everybody out there. We could see them beyond the cow lot, and Orla told us she could do some business from back across the way.

There was fencing to rest her rifle on, and she took out a fat white guy first. It was hard to know if they were all drunk or just naturally demented, especially once Orla had hit a brave in the head that sent gravy everywhere. That bunch just whooped and yelped and seemed a fair bit more excited, and that would be the white boys and savages together.

The one-eared Indian even saw fit to climb down off his pony so he could scalp the fat white guy Orla had shot and killed.

"That's some bunch," I said once I saw what he was up to.

That fellow held the scalp high and hooted, climbed on his horse again and took off.

"Mine," I told them and lit out after him without a thought or reservation. I headed off at a gallop like that was something I'd been born to do.

Orla kept firing. I could hear the hooting and yodeling thinning out as I left the clearing and plunged into a patch of piney woods. There was a time when I would have been cautious about it and worried over my safety, but the past few months had just about killed off all my fretfulness.

Of course, that was my first time chasing a one-eared Indian into the woods, a brave I knew was on a tear of killing all sorts of people, and I'd just watched him claim the scalp off one of his friends. Old me would have gone the other way and would have had good reason for it, but new me who'd crossed the prairie into the foothills of the Rockies and had been running desperados to ground for a livelihood just slowed my horse to a walk and looked every direction I could until I'd spied that Indian's pony up ahead.

The trouble with Indians, the mean ones anyway, was that they were awfully cagey and would come at you in ways you were too white even to guess at to good effect. So I was low in the saddle and gazing around to try to see where he went since the only thing up ahead of me, I could tell by then, was his pony. He had to be in there somewhere, and I found out just where once he'd jumped.

He came dropping on me out of a tree. Of course, he did a spot of yelping. I don't know if he was Comanche or not, but he sure got up to their brand of business. He yipped and wailed and crashed into me with his big, bloody knife in hand. I would have been gutted and done for if my horse hadn't reared and shucked him. Of course, I didn't have hold enough to keep from sailing off as well.

Thinking back, I remember the stink of him chiefly. He had scalps hanging off him, most of them ripe, and he was greasy and filthy as well. I felt like I'd fallen into a bear den and was grappling for my life.

He clearly meant to kill me and take some pleasure in it. He was grunting and saying Indian stuff while I focused on his knife hand and did everything I could to keep his blade out from between my ribs. That was no easy thing because he was powerful and ropey, and I felt sure he'd had a lot of practice knifing folks to death.

While we rolled around in the dirt and pine needles, he

closed in and bit me hard, so I sank my teeth into what
I could reach of him, but he just hooted and howled. He
wasn't in pain. The man was amused, and I think that's
when he stabbed me. I can't be altogether certain because
I'd never been stabbed before and wasn't clear on what I
might be feeling down around my ribs.

After the initial prick and pain, I can recall an odd
sensation of something being in me where nothing should
have been. But then it was gone when he pulled his blade.
He went all Indian showy and licked it. That gave me time
enough to find my Colt. I didn't even try to pull it out of
the holster but just rolled back enough to aim clear of my
leg. The first shot caught the shoulder of his knifing arm.
The second one hit him in the breastbone, and that bullet
leaving the pistol put a crease across my thigh.

So I shot him mostly but myself a little too. Even still
he didn't die like maybe a decent fellow would have.
Being more beast than man, he crawled around and tried
to finish me off. His knife, though, had gotten too heavy
for him, and he was carrying a pistol that he lacked the
strength to raise, especially after I'd shot him a third time.
He still wouldn't quit moving, so I put a fourth bullet in
him, and I don't recall being bothered a bit.

That last one did for him, and where those bullets
passed through, he was a grisly mess, which didn't keep me
from kicking him twice once I'd managed to find my feet.
Then I staggered to my pony, got up on her somehow and
headed back toward the clearing and the cow lot.

It was quiet over there by the time I arrived, and Orla
and them were sorting corpses over by a shed. She'd picked

off every last one just standing at the fencerow. I could smell the whiskey riding up and guessed they'd been too drunk, most of them, to know who was shooting at them and from where.

Ira handed me up a flyer he'd pulled out of one of them's pocket. Their sort seemed to carry those things like calling cards. I guess if they went to rob or kill somebody and didn't inspire sufficient quaking, they could show their likeness on a handbill and thereby get some fear stirred up.

This one had been a Messick with an ambitious history of carnage committed on both people and livestock. He was only good for sixty dollars, which he'd probably found provoking right up until Orla relieved him of half his head.

I looked around at that bunch, sprawled in the mud. She'd caught them in pertinent places. That probably hadn't been much of a challenge for her since they'd all been standing around drunk.

I remember feeling sad, or low at least, and asking Ira, "What did we just do?"

I think he told me back, "What you wanted," before he noticed I was bleeding and called Orla and the rest of them over. That's when I fell off of my horse.

I remember hardly anything after that aside from the odd jab of pain and a nagging sense of sweaty discomfort. I was aware sometimes we were traveling, moving along the wagon road, and somebody had done me the service of tying me onto Gunther. The way he walked, the way he smelled, reminded me of home.

Then I thought I was fishing, sitting out in the sun and

talking to the cousin I used to go to the river with. He
didn't make any sense, and I didn't make much, and our
lines weren't even in the water.

"I could drink some of that," I told him. And somebody
from somewhere put a damp rag to my lips.

It went like that for a while. In and out. Light and dark.
Gunther dander and his easy walk. The odd ache. Sweat
running into my eyes. And then nothing for a stretch until
I finally woke up.

I was in somebody's bed, and I'd not been on a mattress
lately. There was proper linen and a coverlet, and all of
it smelled like flowers and lye. The ceiling above me was
painted planking. The table beside me was topped with
marble and had a fancy brass oil lamp on it and a Bible
that appeared to have been long held and read.

Light streamed in from a window. I'd never been in a
nicer room. Ours weren't painted back at home but just
raw planking straight from the mill.

Then I heard somebody down toward the foot. I had to
raise up to see her, and that only went about half as well
as I'd hoped. I was weak and sore. Feverish, I guess. There
was a woman back in the corner. She looked at me once
she'd given over staring at the wall.

I decided she'd probably been a pretty woman before
she'd gotten spoiled, before whatever sickness she was
struggling with had taken hold and reduced her. She was
drawn and pale and wearing what looked like a white sack
of dress. It draped to the floor and swallowed her so that
she was just head and hands.

"Where is this?" I asked her.

She took a step toward me. She laughed, and then she wept.

Devil Up

1

I'd been in the care, I came to find out, of a man who was kind of a doctor, but then he was kind of a dentist too and even did a bit of baking when the cookhouse had need of him. I do know he sewed me up and mixed an elixir for me, and I met him once I was back to my regular self when he came around.

"Ah," he said upon seeing me awake. "The luck was with you," he told me. "That knife missed a lot of stuff."

His name was Percy and something German I couldn't quite wrap my mouth around, and he'd been on his way to somewhere else, had come out west from Boston, when three gentlemen (he called them) relieved him of his belongings and his horse.

"I got to watch them hang," he told me while he examined my wound.

That was the first time I'd seen it out from under the bandage, and it was bright red and puffy and seeping. It didn't strike me as the kind of wound a lucky man would have.

"I started doctoring on Ruben's missus and stuck around."

He looked across the room, so I looked too. She was over in the corner where I'd first spied her. I'd noticed since then that she haunted that spot. She'd grimed up the wall and picked at the planking, would stand hours there making her noises and messing around.

"She lost two babies," Doc Percy told me. "Then had one for two years, but he died."

She swung our way and then swung back. I heard her moan a little.

"You can't help her?"

"That's her helped," he said.

"Am I in her bed?"

He shook his head. "She curls up on the floor."

"My friends around?" I asked the doc.

"Come and go. You've been laid up here most of a week." He poked at my wound in a robust way, and I complained colorfully about it. "One of them's here. Been here," he said and pointed at the door before calling out, "Come on in."

I hoped it wasn't Arturo after a week of thinking up poetry, but I felt like before I even saw her it would have to be Belle. It was, and nobody had prettied her up. She had on the ratty clothes she favored, and her boots were muddy up to her ankles. Her hair was the usual tangled mess, but I still felt like I was seeing the best looking thing I ever would.

"Hey," I told her.

She tooted back.

"She doesn't talk." I explained to Percy she had the gear for it and all.

He winked at Belle. "Doesn't talk to you," he said.

Then he left before I could push him on it. He reminded me to drink his elixir, announced he had two teeth to pull, and was out the door and gone.

"What was that about?" I asked Belle, but still she only tooted back before she parked herself on the edge of my bed and made me show her my wound. The doc had stitched it shut with thread and had made a neat job of it, but aside from his tidy work, that wound was an awful thing to see. Red and moist and hot to the touch, draining wherever it could.

"He says I'm lucky," I told Belle.

She had a toot for that as well and then left me to go where Ruben's missus was over in her corner. She was facing the wall, and Belle stood close and waited for her to turn. She did in a while and laughed Belle's way before weeping Belle's way too until Belle consoled the woman by taking one hand in both of hers.

The rest of them were around. Arturo, and Ira, and Pawnee boy had set up camp by a branch about a mile outside Alma while Orla was passing her nights in a back room of the jailhouse because Ruben was worried those men she'd shot to pieces might have friends. He didn't care if those friends got hold of the rest of us. He was fixed on Orla's safety and gave her the bed he usually took.

Ruben must have needed a sane companion. I wasn't inclined to blame him for it and couldn't imagine too many acceptable candidates found their way to Alma, certainly awfully few with the charm and looks of the lady who'd come with us. I wanted to warn him, though, that she'd shift off him just like she'd shifted off the husband she'd traveled with to Oneida in order to take up with Arturo who she'd shifted off of too.

All Ruben had to do was ask her about it, and Orla would own up to the pattern. I'd talked it over with her. She knew she liked to move through men, but I imagine Sheriff Ruben was like the rest of us around and had decided he had the stuff it'd take to break her. Most men are ripe to believe they're not like anybody else.

So we already weren't the same bunch before I got healed up, and that took longer than I'd been hoping for, even with the doc's elixir. It was greasy and tasted like pine sap with a dash of toe grit in it, so knocking my daily dose of it back wasn't much of a delight. Maybe it helped in the end, or maybe nature simply took her course. All I know is I got less sore and red and puffy after a while, and the pus or whatever I'd been leaking all dried up and quit in time.

It was mostly just me in Ruben's house with his afflicted wife, whose name was Angeline. I came to learn the woman and Ruben were sweethearts back in Missouri where Ruben was meant to go into business with her brother but changed his mind. Instead, he brought her west and got somehow into the lawman trade along with winning a saloon and a hotel playing cards.

They were going to raise a family in the community of Alma, but Angeline couldn't manage to deliver a child alive. Then when she did, he died as well, and she came to believe she was poisoned inside.

"Cursed in the womb." That's how the doc put it, and he allowed he'd tried every way he knew to tell her she was wrong. "Life's hard out here. Stuff can't all live. Now she won't go near a man."

"I worry about Orla," I confessed to the doc, by which I meant I worried about Ruben, or by which I proba-bly actually meant I worried about Angeline. She might have been down on her womb and off of men, but I had to think she could still locate some way to feel betrayed. Then what might she do since the woman already was living in a corner of a room?

The rest of them started coming to visit once they had clearance for it. The doc would tell Ruben what was per-mitted, and he'd ride herd on that, so at first they only popped in for the quickest of hey howdys, but it got to where I could hold up through a conversation in time.

Orla was first, and Ruben came with her. I noticed he had a kind word for his wife in her corner that he deliv-ered from the middle of the room. She made one of her noises in response and kept turned to the wall like she'd been. Orla didn't appear to even notice the woman but sat at my bedside smiling and filling me in on the trip we'd made from that cow lot full of dead men back down the wagon road to Alma.

"One night I thought you were lost to us," she told me, and it seemed like something tender might follow. "But you were just thinking hard," she said, "before you messed your pants."

Then Orla told me two of the men she'd shot we'd actually cashed in. "Arturo went and found your Indian and killed him a little more."

Ira swung by for a visit after that, and while he was happy and all to see me on the mend, he had a few other things on his mind. Sitting still in one spot had given him time to do a load of thinking. Like any sensible man, Ira wondered how much more desperado hunting he could do.

"It weighs on me," is how he put it.

I felt like I knew what he meant. We'd gotten up as a bunch to some troubling business for the sake of a bounty or two and done things you'd want to put from your mind but couldn't, at least not entirely.

"What might you do?" I asked him.

"Thinking I'll meet my brother in Abilene."

When Arturo came, he brought Pawnee boy, but Pawnee boy wouldn't come into the house. That was chiefly due to the fact he'd never been in a proper house before and couldn't see any reason to break his string. Instead, he stood outside and looked in one of my windows for a bit until that maybe struck him as more domesticated than he wanted. I just know he was there one moment, but the next moment he was gone.

Arturo was less torn up about Orla and Ruben than I'd expected, but that was because he was romantic, and they can make use of everything. So he had chunks of verse to share for all the sad and tragic parts and poetry too for anything hopeful that happened to spring to mind. That'd be in addition to how he went on about jousting for Orla's affection with a worthy fellow, Arturo told me, as fine and comely as a Greek god.

I got the feeling halfway in that Arturo was torn between loving Orla and Ruben since, being a romantic, he could make room for both of them in his heart.

Soon enough Arturo came around to laying out Pawnee boy's story. Until then, I hadn't suspected there was awfully much to tell. I'd figured him for one of those shiftless Indian braves nobody would really miss, which was why Pawnee boy and his homely dog could end up stuck with me and Belle. He could stay where he was or he could go, and none of those Pawnees really cared.

Arturo, though, sat by my bed and straightened me out on Pawnee boy. They'd had the leisure for several heart-to-hearts, and Pawnee boy had confessed to Arturo he'd been tapped to be a berdache and hadn't believed he'd enjoy that much.

"A what?"

"A two-spirit. A would-be woman."

For Pawnees in particular and Indians generally, there was usually somebody in a tribe who lived as a third thing. Not a man and not a woman but kind of in between. In Pawnee boy's tribe, their berdache had died with no warning, and they were caught without a junior berdache to step in and take the reins. It seems there was talk among the elders, and Pawnee boy got designated because the rest of the braves were needed for hunting and war parties and such while Pawnee boy drank root liquor and did more laying around than was seemly.

"What does a berdache do?" I asked Arturo.

He talked around it for a bit, but I got the feeling a berdache loved up women when he wasn't loving up men.

Then Arturo got around to his own plans. He guessed he should head back to Mexico and check up on his wife and kids.

It was a week more still before the doc turned me loose, and I needed a couple of days beyond that to get where I was steady. In truth, I was feeling better than I let on because I wasn't in any hurry to go back to sleeping on the ground. But soon enough there wasn't any help for it, and me and Belle left Angeline to her corner and rode both on her bay out of town to the branch where Arturo and Ira and Pawnee had been living for a stretch.

That camp site looked it. There were clothes drying on the bushes and firewood piled up like they weren't sure they would ever leave. Bones were scattered everywhere from animals they'd eaten, and they'd left the wind to take the trash they'd made wherever it liked.

"Hell, boys," I told them once I'd seen the place. It was a sight that made me pucker because I was the sort who was constantly nipping loose threads or oiling my guns.

It turned out the state of the place was the outer version of what was happening inside because Ira and Pawnee boy, Arturo too, were working through impulses and complicated motivations. They hadn't any of them truly decided what their next steps ought to be and so were doing all kinds of dithering and mess making while they gauged impulses. That was the first time I truly felt like the boss and the colonel that they needed. They were good about doing what you told them they ought to, but they weren't terribly much use until you'd laid out your decree.

"All right then," is how I started, "we're not going on like this."

It helped me too because you have your doubts after you've been wounded. I had an uncle who'd fought in Tennessee and lost pretty much all of his hand. A Minni ball caught him and took most of it but for half his thumb. So he had a curious nub at the end of his arm that served as a reminder not just that he'd fought but also that bullets had a way of ripping flesh. You start believing this world is maybe organized to do you in.

That's how it feels once you've had a bullet through you or a knife between your ribs. You might have gone around believing you were sturdy and built to last, but then you've gone and run across a contradiction. I tried to come off being tough and certain, but I'd had a knife in between my liver and my spleen and so had a hard time believing I was sturdy anymore.

I'd thought of my uncle with the thumb while laying up in Ruben's house and how all of his people would laugh and marvel at how careful he'd become, how leery he was about doing all the stuff he used to do. I felt like I'd come to understand him laying in that bed with only Ruben's damaged wife for a companion. It was as if the cover had all been stripped away, and I could see the harm ahead. But you're shot or you're stabbed or you're weak from fever, and you don't know how to meet it.

So I started with the baby step of cleaning that camp

site up and getting it fit for civilized people to eat and
sleep as long as they had to. Then Belle went off and came
back with two brook trout, the sort of trick she'd pulled so
often we'd stopped even wondering how.

I could hardly remember the bed I'd slept in after two
nights by the branch, and I well knew it was time for us
to figure out our business. It seemed likely to me we'd be
splitting up and heading off where we pleased. That was
the general feeling anyway until Orla and Ruben came
calling with a fresh batch of rascals. A stack of new flyers
had come in on the stage.

"Don't know how you're tending," Ruben told us, "but
I was thinking these might help." He handed those handbills over and then stood by to talk us through them.

We'd picked up trash and organized clothes and had
nothing otherwise going and so passed around the things
as Ruben told us who was who. They were mostly new to
us even though we'd been tracking their sort for a while.
So you would have thought we might have recognized
various hangers on, but there was clearly an endless supply
of depravity afoot. Aside from the Goins brothers—who'd
added a marshal and four deputies to their body count
and so were worth three hundred dollars if you wanted to
take the chance—the rest of them were thieves of money,
thieves of cattle, thieves of horses, and more than a few of
them had killed folks who'd simply gotten in their way.

There was no imagination to much of it, just people
who took what they wanted and shot down whoever they
needed to. It was a sad and tedious commentary on the
flavor of life out there and a going piece of commerce for

people willing to do what we did. Or willing anyway to take on the sort of work that we'd been doing. I wasn't sure there was money enough to put us on the wagon road again.

I knew I wasn't in any personal state to do much deciding, so I just looked over those flyers and handed them on so that Ira and Arturo and Pawnee boy could see what was loose on the land. Orla, oddly enough, was the one who was most enthusiastic. At first, I figured she was bucking us up to help get us clear of Alma so she could stay behind with Ruben unencumbered and baggage free. Arturo appeared to have made a kind of peace with losing his woman, or at the very least he was able to seem prepared to go on living and could make civilized chat with Ruben and manage the odd smile Orla's way.

It probably helped that Orla and Ruben didn't display much affection. He had a damaged wife back home after all, and so even by Alma standards, Ruben was going to have to treat his new Irish girlfriend and her freckled decolletage with more than a hint of gentlemanly circumspection for a while. That appeared to come easy to him because he was naturally decent, which helped tamp Arturo's venom down because he was decent too.

Then Orla announced that she'd ride out with us on one last sweep along the trail to see if we couldn't top up our kitty before we divided the shares. That was enough to tempt Arturo, of course, and he brought on Pawnee boy and Ira who had been hanging around and living like tramps for longer than they'd liked.

So here was an actual thing to do that we could all get

paid for, but before I could nod and throw in with them, Belle walked over to Arturo and picked up one of his hands far enough so she could press her forehead to it. Then she didn't snort exactly but just sighed and let it go.

2

I got the feeling this whole last hunt was Orla's gift to Arturo, a chance for him to work out whatever he had to to turn her loose. So she was chummy with him, and he was sentimental with her. He kept remembering what they'd been through and reminding her about it, and she'd tolerate him at it until he'd start veering on forlorn.

But then after a night or two of staying clear, she got back under the blanket with him because Orla, at bottom, was a woman with a nagging use for men. She wasn't bashful about it. I'll give her that. She could be as randy as a cowhand, though Orla did appear to have her standards where it came to the quality of her men. She liked them dashing or, at the very least, as pretty as Sheriff Ruben, but it was easy to tell she wasn't a lady who'd stick with one for long.

I approved of that about her. Back then, men were usually the louts and scoundrels, but Orla was a forward-thinking woman who turned that on its head. She also had a way with a rifle like nobody I'd seen, so I didn't care whose blanket she crawled under as long as she picked off rascals from a hundred yards away.

I guess it was like old times for a bit. We all had our parts, and we played them. We moved along the wagon trail and chatted up whoever we found. We had seven or eight hundred dollars-worth of criminals running loose, a mix of rustlers and murderers and one trio of bank robbers who'd killed half of some town in Texas with an overabundance of dynamite.

Two of them were brothers, and the other was a friend of theirs from Kansas where they'd all grown up and gotten tired of farming wheat and corn. I know all of this because they told us when we found them. A couple of them were down a well, and the other was topside in a tizzy because he couldn't figure how to haul them up.

We got clued in when that boy tried to pay us for help with a wad of half burnt money.

"What happened to this?" I asked him.

"Hell, I guess we blowed it up."

They weren't bright, those three. The two in the well had gone down after water before they'd troubled themselves to come up with a plan for climbing out.

Gunther had snaked whole tree trunks out of mountain hollows, so snatching two Kansas dullards out of a well wasn't much of a chore for him. Those boys were so grateful that they gave us their guns after Orla had asked to see them. She just told them she had an interest in pistols, that handling them stirred her up. So she soon had their guns, and that's when she showed them their flyer from our stack.

Arturo had to read it to them. Those three had never been big on learning, and they objected to the drawing of them, which did those boys no favors and made them look, somehow, even duller than they were. They were also quick to say their list of crimes was incomplete and told us everything they'd been up to since they're handbill had been printed.

"This ain't so bad," one of the two who'd been in the well informed us. "Out of dynamite, just about. Half decided to go back home."

The other two nodded. They all seemed to think they'd get let off because they were only lunks from Kansas who were done with bank robbing and could finally see the abiding allure of the farm.

We headed to Fairplay to cash them in, and for the two days that we had them, those boys talked about all the business they'd get up to back in Kansas once whoever we were taking them to would see clear to turn them out.

I still remember the look on their faces when the sheriff down in Fairplay and a couple of his deputies jerked those boys around.

"Y'all want to keep going?" Ira asked us. By then, we had a solid chunk of money to divvy up, but the company was good and the future unsettled, and Orla and Arturo seemed to be enjoying their little fling, so we turned north

and all agreed we'd make a run up to Blue River, and then
turn back south to Alma, and that would be enough for
us.

So we had a plan with a route to take and a goal, which
served to ease my mind a bit, since it's wearing after a
while to lead a life that's open-ended. I might have been
only sixteen, but even I was tired. Some of that was probably due to how I'd had a knife stuck in me, but plenty of it
was on account of we'd just been wandering around.

A last jaunt to Blue River and then back down to Alma
struck me as a satisfying capstone. I didn't care if we didn't
pick up any scoundrels on the way. We could use the trip
to work out who'd be heading where and why. It would
give us the chance to maybe bust apart like we'd come together, which is to say gradually and over a piece of time.
Ira had been talking like he was ready to head for Abilene,
while Arturo would maybe visit his real wife down in
Mexico and try to put from his mind what Orla was getting up to in Colorado.

That left me and Belle and Pawnee boy to figure out
our plans. I felt responsible for both of them because I
was built that way. It had started out just me and Gunther
clear out to the plains where I'd picked up Belle and Pawnee boy like brambles on my trousers. So all of a sudden
it was me and Gunther, that homely dog, and them. That
gave me a duty, I did believe, to take charge of their wel-
fare. That meant they were welcome to go where I went,
and I'd never resent them for it because fate or something
out there had put us in each other's way.

That trip up the wagon trail to Blue River gave us time

to get used to the future, and as soon as we stopped caring if we ran across more rascals, that sort of criminal trash was all we saw.

We were two days north of Alma when we just about got bushwhacked by two fellows, and they might have been trouble if one of the bushwhacker's pistols hadn't blown up. It misfired and half-exploded, blinded him in both his eyes. Being scum, of course, he blamed us for it since we'd had the temerity to come along and strike him as inviting.

He wasn't any problem to control, if you could tolerate his whining, but his partner led me and Ira on a chase up through the woods. We were in the vicinity of a place they called Mt. Lincoln, were down at the bottom and dogging a man who'd decided to run to the top. He shot at us every now and again, about thirty feet too high, and then he gave out of bullets and yelled for a while before he seemed to make a strategic decision to carry on in silence. He even got crafty enough to take off his yellow bandana and use it to shift us off his course by tying it to a tree.

Those two were only worth sixty dollars together, so me and Ira stopped in the midst of it all to have a think and catch our breath.

We could hear him. He was way up the slope and sounded like a herd of deer. He was crashing through the underbrush and panting and chuffing and grunting. After we'd stood there and listened to him a bit, we didn't even need to talk but both turned around and headed down the way we'd just come up.

Ira told me about growing up down around New Orleans. He allowed he couldn't remember why he'd left it anyway.

I remembered what I'd put behind and still had a grip on why.

"Dirt floor," I told him. "Chickens inside. Pig sometimes when he wanted, and too many people, most of them only living for moonshine after a while." I couldn't say where I'd end up, but it wouldn't be back there.

By the time we'd returned to Orla and them, the boy with the pistol that misfired was dead and wrapped in a blanket. There was a part of me that didn't even want to ask them what had happened because we'd all been around each other so long I knew they wouldn't lie.

"He got lippy," Orla volunteered. "Went for a knife or something."

I could imagine the man being upset his pistol had misfired and could even picture him lashing out and maybe reaching for a blade, but he couldn't see and wasn't about to do harm to sensible people. All he'd offered was a chance for Orla and them to make him easier to tote.

That's about where we'd come to since we'd started chasing around after scoundrels. Some of it at first had been about bringing wayward men (and women) to justice, but it seemed to me we were a bunch anymore that was only cashing them in. We weren't terribly much better than Dupree and his boys and were sort of following their example since everybody they brought in was always dead.

Pawnee boy offered to take off through the woods and up the mountain to see if he could locate the partner, but I told him that fellow was probably up and over the knob by then.

That prompted Pawnee boy to answer back with his favorite scrap English. "Howdy," is what he told me, and then he spat.

Orla said they'd talked to a lady who'd passed by on a donkey, and she told them about a camp full of no goods by a lake a few miles out where that lady said we were sure to find all the villainous trash we wanted.

"They killed a pile of ranching people," is what the woman told them. "Scalped some of them. Made off with all of their cows."

Orla said she asked if it was Indians, which would have been of no interest to us. They didn't try Indians and hang them out there but just killed them at first sight and certainly didn't bother with a bounty. You might have gotten two dollars for Sitting Bull, but they treated the rest like snakes.

The woman said it was whites and Indians, which was becoming a kind of thing.

"Did she pick any of them out?" I asked, and Orla handed me two flyers.

One featured a man with ambitious sideburns, the kind you grew even back then on a bet, and the other one appeared to be some brand of woman who went by the name Big Ruthie, but this creature had sort of a moustache and one eye that had been sewn shut. Also Big Ruthie had busted out of a jailhouse up in the Front Range and was said to have chewed off the ears of a deputy before she made him properly dead.

I remembered Big Ruthie from the various times I'd

sifted through our stack, but I'd never expected to know the chance to see that lady in person because I thought she was maybe the handbill makers having a bit of fun.

"We can slip in for a look," Orla said. "Pull out if it's more than we want."

I pretended like that could be something that might happen, but I'd never known us to pull out of anything before, and I imagined we'd just hang back while Orla did some shooting. There was no flinch at all to Orla when there were scoundrels to put down.

Then we had to find the lake, and that was no easy matter because the woman on the donkey had given it out as "over yonder." She'd pointed, like folks will at the horizon or the sun in the sky. So we rode on and looked for people to ask, but folks out there were scarce.

We passed two abandoned homesteads. They had cabins and cow lots on them, but everything was empty and stripped down with no people who weren't in the ground. Those folks might have been driven off or they could have just given up. By then, winter was closing in, and you could tell it'd be a trial. I'd broken out my buffalo hat and was finding Yasper's buckskin jacket not quite warm enough.

After about half a day, we came in sight of a kind of way station, a shack made mostly out of slab wood where you could sit by a fire for a while, have a drink of something and a piece of a pig, buy maybe a bit of wagon tack if your gear had given out, and pay the man inside about three times what it was worth.

This one was called Nesbits. That was painted on the

side of the place, and I volunteered to go in and see about
that lake while the rest of them stayed well back and out
sight so as to not be a hindrance to rascals riding in.

It's hard now for folks to even imagine how awful spots
like Nesbits were. There wasn't any light to speak of beyond one window covered with sacking and the low glow
of a fire nobody had bothered to feed in a while. The mer-
chandise they offered was shoved into cubbies or piled up
on a table, but clearly the attraction of the place was the
bar where the whiskey was served.

More a plank really held up by a couple of cottonwood
trunks, and there were three men leaning on it drinking
out of coffee cups. They all shifted enough to squint my
way. The guy behind the bar just grunted.

"Y'all got a lake around here?" I asked them about as
boyishly as I could but that didn't keep the man at the bar
from setting a cup out for me. He poured a half inch of
something in it and said to me, "Two bits."

"All right." I paid him. I sniffed. I drank. It tasted like it
had been brewed in a boot. I guessed I'd be blind in a little
while or I wouldn't.

"Going fishing, arc you?" one of the customers asked
me. Him and the other two had a laugh.

"Looking for my uncle," I told them. I described his
ambitious sideburns. "Called him Higby back home. Can't
say what he's latched to now."

"Might be I know him," one of them said.

I'm aware now the fellow talking to me was a notorious
rascal who'd do anything to anybody if he saw some profit
in it, but he wasn't keen, like most of the rest of them, to

be famous for stuff he'd done. He was that rare bird out
there who'd get up carnage, engage in a whole slew of it,
and then let other scoundrels with more natural climb lay
claim to having done it while he laid back being wicked
with no itch at all to boast. He almost seemed gentle. That
was his gift and helped to put him right up on you before
you'd figured out what he was.

"Come on. I'll take you out there."

He walked outside and left me to follow. We rode at a
walk for a bit. He asked where I was coming from, how
long I'd been out on the trail, and I gave him back whatever I thought would work for me and fit.

"When did you last see your uncle?" he wanted to know.

I had a fair bit to say about Higby, my mother's brother
and more of a roughneck than he could keep bottled up.

We took a branch trail off into the woods, and that's
where he fell behind me. He kept talking, but I couldn't
see what he was getting up to back there. I also couldn't
be sure that Orla and them were anywhere nearby, so I
guessed if things went bad, it was going to be just me and
him.

That fellow was doing a heck of a job trying to keep
me at ease. He had a world of ready chat that he'd call up
and visit on me, and if I'd been anybody else in any other
line, I don't doubt I would have ended up dead. But I'd
been chasing people like him for a while and had only just
recovered from a stabbing, so I was more ready to believe
the worst about him than most people would have been.

I was only hoping he wasn't the sort who'd shoot me
in the back, but I had an instinct he was too cocksure for

something like that and would instead work to win my trust and make me suffer for it.

"Ain't no Higby," is what he told me. Then he eased his horse up beside me so I could see the knife in his hand.

It was even bigger than the knife that one-eared Indian had skewered me with, and he had a chance there for a second or two to lean in and lay me open, but the man enjoyed it all a little too much. He wanted me feeling terrified. That seemed to be something he savored, so I told him, "Wait," and told him, "Don't," while he gave me a folksy wink.

"Awful sorry."

He was drawing back to get a little force behind the blade when I caught him flush on the forehead with my hammer. I'd found it among those dead missionaries just before I'd claimed my boots, and I'd long carried it in my saddle bag because I've never been one for a knife. It takes a certain brand of savage moxy to stick a blade in a man but something well short of that to tap one with a hammer.

So I hit him once and hit him again and hit him another time and just kept at it until he'd tumbled off his horse. That took longer than I'd expected. He was splashing on me by then.

I stayed where I was and wiped myself off. I calmed his horse and took her reins. I heard Pawnee boy yipping and riding up. He was Indian and couldn't help that he enjoyed bloodletting so much. I wasn't about to hold it against him, but I didn't much care to join in.

The rest of them came along just behind him.

"He with that bunch at the lake?" Ira asked me.

"Probably. Ought to be up here, I guess."

We left him where he was, all battered and pulpy. I knew from the look Belle gave me, I might be digging a hole in a while. At first, though, we had other business, and I continued the way we'd been going.

We saw sunshine on water right when we were thinking we might best give up looking, and we left our horses and walked up to where the trees quit at the bank. That lake was wooded just about all around and had some size to it. You'd be wanting a boat to make it clear across. There was a point of land that jutted out about eighty yards along the way, and that appeared to be where the bunch we'd heard about had settled in.

They had canvas stretched out where they could and tepees here and there. A couple of them were wrestling in the dirt while six or eight more sat watching. We didn't see the one with the fishing pole until after he'd seen us. He was down our way parked on a stump with his bare feet in the water, and he whistled and waved to warn his buddies while he pointed in our direction. Orla's direction actually. She'd, like usual, taken the lead and was too far out in the clear to help but attract some notice.

The guy with the pole had a gun at hand too, and he pulled it out and fired in our direction. Orla's direction, Arturo decided, and so got gentlemanly in his way. That is to say he pulled his smokewagon, shouted something indignant, and let loose a couple of rounds.

Arturo was far more poetical and romantic than coordinated, so he wasn't about to shoot close to a man sitting on a stump, but that fellow was no slouch with a gun, and he just needed one shot for Arturo and caught him in a spot between his shoulder and his neck.

Arturo grunted as the bullet went through. He staggered and, naturally, declaimed. He came out with something in Spanish that went on for a bit before he switched to English and told us he'd wager he was done for.

Orla in particular wasn't about to tolerate that and shoved Arturo with the rifle barrel to make him both shut up and move.

It took three of us to get him onto his horse, and I kept hold of the reins and pulled him with us out of the woods while he slumped onto his saddle. Every now and then he'd hit me with a couplet or something like it, which I took to mean Arturo was maybe less done for than he'd thought.

They were chasing of course, the ones who weren't too drunk to ride, and that included the guy with the fishing pole who hadn't bothered to put his boots on. He was mounted on a donkey that flat tore through the woods.

We weren't going to outrun them. That was plain enough to me. Orla as well, so we sent the rest of them on out towards the trail. We gave them our horses to lead and found a spot where a couple of trees had come down, big pines we could aim from and hide behind. I had to share mine with a rattlesnake that didn't want the company. All I could do was discourage him with a stick.

He didn't care for that either and rattled at me, coiled and struck a couple of times. I don't know if it was because I'd hung around too long with Arturo, but instead of getting fed up with that snake and blowing off his head, I made time to take in my predicament in a sort of romantic way. There I was caught between a pack of irate scoundrels and a venomous reptile with nothing to do but try and fight my way out. I figured there had to be a pile of poetry about that sort of thing. Of course, I also didn't want to get bit by a rattler, so I shortly came to my regular senses and killed that snake with a pine limb. It seemed likely to me romantic thinking was what got Arturo shot.

Orla wasn't one to mess around where it came to shooting people. Once she'd decided you were some brand of villain, she'd take a bead and bring you down. Our fix just then made it easy on her since everybody but us was worth shooting, so she steadied and started by knocking that fellow off his mule. Then she shot him again as he squirmed because he'd put a round through her man of the moment. The rest of them she only shot once and moved along.

I fired a few times. I think I hit people. I know I put one of the Indians down. That one-eared brave who'd knifed me had kind of soured me on their lot, which I wasn't proud of and hoped I'd find the leisure to get over, but just then I was leaving the white men for Orla and seeking the Indians out.

She probably didn't need my help with any of that bunch because once Orla got going, she was a regular angel of death. There was no pity to the woman. No doubt. No merciful second chances. I found my targets and fired when I could while she just mowed them down. She'd go back and finish off the ones she'd not hit where she wanted. There was no getting off by playing dead. There was no crawling away. The only ones who lived of that bunch were the ones too drunk to mount up and come.

By the time we'd found our way out to the trail, Arturo was barely awake, and Ira and them had torn up a shirt and wrapped his wound tight with it. We were two hard days from Alma and the only medical man around, so we pushed south and stopped once to feed and sleep for a couple of hours. The weather was turning, and it was cold in the dark, which we decided was good for Arturo and might keep him from bleeding out or pussing up.

That's what we told ourselves anyway, and once we started seeing landmarks, we sent Ira ahead to Alma to find the doc and get him primed. In the meantime, Pawnee boy was treating Arturo with a poultice, which appeared to be mud and switchgrass that he'd chewed on for a while. It didn't seem to be improving things or making them worse either. Arturo had a fever, and his wound was a ghastly sight, so nobody complained when Pawnee boy spackled it over and hid it.

The doc had a room in the stable in Alma where he would sleep sometimes, and he directed us to take Arturo in and leave him on the bunk.

Beyond the poultice, Arturo got elixir as well and some sort of sulphur powder, and it was all enough to make us believe Arturo might pull through. We all took turns sitting with him, even Sheriff Ruben. Not that Arturo would have noticed. He wasn't awake awfully much.

I remember going in for a visit with Belle the day after we'd returned, and I could tell by the sounds she made and the way she tugged at Arturo's blanket that, while he might hold on for a little while, he'd surely be dead soon. Even short of a spasm, Belle could always give the game away.

I doubt Arturo went out like he'd hoped to, with a cry maybe and couplet, but instead he just sweated and mumbled and gave up in the small hours the next night. He had for company just then a Pawnee castoff and an octoroon. They didn't wake us up to tell us but let the doc come around with the news.

We were camping hard by, and it was only me, Belle, and Gunther and the horses. Doc took a cup of the coffee I offered, perched on a rock, and shook his head. We knew why he was there and so didn't require anything more than that.

I think of that doc sometimes still and the little he would say, which was usually all you'd need to hear and routinely just enough. I've got a doctor now who explains everything, even sometimes draws me pictures and gives me the Latin for the various complaints I have. It doesn't help. I don't feel better, and there's nothing in it like a cure. I'd be just as well served with him nodding from a rock.

We all took turns digging Arturo's hole, even the doc and Belle and Ruben. Orla made a fine show of being something like a widow for a day.

None of us quite knew what to say about Arturo, but I felt like me and Ira and probably even Orla and Pawnee boy were all thinking nearly the same thing. I knew Arturo could be me. He could be any of us if we kept at the sort of business we'd been up to. Yes, you made a little money for a while, but the odds were good for getting dead because people were awfully free with bullets out there where we were.

Ruben wished Arturo holy peace and eternal rest as well, and I think we were all about ready to let that serve and be done with it when we got a snatch of poetry to cap off the burial.

"Behold I go where I know infinity to dwell." It was not a voice I recognized or one I'd ever heard. When Belle finished, she tossed a clod in that hit Arturo with a thump. Then she went off on her own and left the churchyard without us.

I thought that might be the start of something, but I never heard her speak again.

3
*

Ira left us first, if you weren't counting Orla. She'd not told us what her plans were, but she'd handed my Winchester back. We'd all had enough. It was mostly a matter of figuring out how to say it, and it proved easy to lay most of it to Arturo in the ground. We knew we'd all end up there eventually, but sooner if we stayed together, so Ira divided up the shares. We were five instead of six, and Pawnee boy had me hold his cash. He didn't know from money. Belle gave me hers too because she was a fairy of the air.

So we only sort of broke up. We all got together to say our goodbyes to Ira who took a pony and a packhorse and planned on steering clear of people on his way to meet his brother in Abilene. I was sad to see him ride off, but we were primed for something else and left Orla with Ruben maybe three days later. If any man could thrive with an infirm wife and a deadeye Irish girlfriend, it was probably Ruben with his chin, his stubble, his pale blue eyes, and his perfect teeth.

He reminded us rascals were loose all up and down the countryside and gave us a box of bullets and a sack of goat jerky. Orla hugged us all and then stood by Ruben and held to his elbow and cried. He consoled her without even one stray time leering at her decolletage. Our homely dog was so weary of traveling, he chose to stay behind with them, and Pawnee boy and Belle both seemed happy enough to let him.

Off we went up the wagon road, the same track we'd been riding for months, but it was just me and Belle and Pawnee boy along with Gunther and a pair of spare horses. Since those two weren't big on conversation, we'd not worked out where we were going, and it was clear they would have followed me to wherever I chose to end up.

That kind of weighed on me. I wasn't in much state to be depended on, and yet there I was with a Pawnee and a girl conceived in sin along with a mule that, given the chance, would stomp my feet or bite me. It wasn't ideal and not at all what I'd pictured back at home when me and Frank and Calvin were first scheming to set out.

I'd dug a fair few holes out there and left men dead on the ground as well, which I can't say I ever got used to, but you'd find a way over and through it because you knew they'd have done for you if you hadn't done for them. That was the sort of balance you struck out there, the bargain you made in your head with what you'd been raised on and all your decent impulses. You couldn't go to court on people or send them a lawyer's letter. Most everything got worked out right away and for good.

So I'd adjusted, let's call it, and doubted I could get back to how I'd been, but I'd half promised myself I wouldn't be shooting people going forward. *Half promised* because I'd make allowances if they needed to get shot. I was hoping out in California we'd get clear of the riff raff and settle into doing regular stuff that didn't call for guns.

We were late in the season to be crossing the mountains. Most everybody we saw on the trail was more than happy to tell us as much, and one guy was even ready to sell us the clothes we'd need for winter. He had coats and trousers and hats and gloves made out of every sort of pelt you could think of, all of them stitched up by his wife and her sister who took Christian care, he told us, with everything they did.

I don't know about that, but we were in dire need of some of what he was selling, and we let him fit us all three out until we were bundled up and warm. He declared to us he'd never before done business with an Indian, and he was giddy about it and insisted on shaking Pawnee boy's hand.

I ended up with rabbit trousers and a coat made out of beaver that was so big and fluffy you could hardly find me inside it if you tried. I had a buffalo hat already and two pair of deerskin gloves, so I was warm in the weather and the other two seemed snug against the wind as well. That convinced me we could probably make it clear up to Breckenridge and lay in there a few months before setting out over the mountains come spring.

We weren't on any kind of clock and were carrying three full shares of money. No folks back home were waiting to hear from us. Nobody ahead was thinking we'd come, so we could cover whatever ground we wanted and stop when we saw fit. On top of that, we were all warm for a change and were fine slowing down and easing along. There's a lot to be said for fighting off a Front Range snow squall in a beaver coat. Gunther wasn't happy about any of it, but unhappy was simply his way.

We camped for maybe a week and a half, got snowed in for a couple of days, and then decided (I did anyway) to make a push for town so we could take a room in Breckinridge and get out of the winter. We were nearly there, maybe twenty miles shy, when trouble finally found us.

I saw them up ahead. Five, maybe six riders who weren't moving up or moving down the trail. Instead, they were spread out across it watching the three of us come. Snow was spitting enough to keep me from seeing exactly what sort they were until we got up to where I could make out a top hat perched on one of them's head.

I figured, at worst, I'd be in for some jawboning since we'd had a scratchy time of it before. That was hardly enough to keep us from going on like we'd been going.

They just sat there and waited until we'd reached them. It was Dupree all right and those boys that rode with him along with a couple of larger fellows I felt like I sort of knew. They were big, those two, and had wild beards on them, bellies out to their saddle horns. Racoon hats, the pair of them, and guns all over the place. I knew I'd seen

them somewhere and supposed it would come to me soon
enough.

"Hey here, sugar," Dupree told Belle.

It was only then that she tooted, and not to him but
more at me. That was all I needed to hear.

We'd walked right up on the Goins brothers, and there
they sat untied and armed. They certainly weren't dead
and strapped to a horse like I'd grown to expect with
Dupree, and he let me look from them to him before he
bothered to clear things up.

"That's right," he said. "We done gone over."

Then one of the Goins brothers announced for anybody
who cared to know it, "I hate a goddamn Indian." He
pulled out a pistol and shot Pawnee boy clean through.

That boy Arturo wounded was the one who fired my
way, and I pitched straight over backwards. I hit my head
on a rock or something and went out cold for a while. It
was dark by the time I woke up, and it was just me and
Pawnee boy laid out on the trail. That Goins had hit him
square in the middle, so he'd probably died in the saddle. I
had to fish myself out of my beaver coat to find out where
I was hit.

That coat probably saved me, it and the buckskin underneath. That boy who shot me couldn't be sure where
I was and where I wasn't, and I was just lucky he was too
lazy to shoot me again. That went for all of them, I had
to think, far too shiftless to climb off their horses. They
just took whatever they could without having to work at it
awfully much. That meant Belle and all our horses. Everything anyway but for Gunther. He must have gone off

through the woods to save his sorry self because he came wandering out and onto the trail once he'd seen me get to my feet.

Dupree's bullet had done little more than scrape off a plug of skin. I was bleeding from it, but the frigid air had helped to stop me up, and Gunther was hauling enough wadding and mess that I could make a proper bandage.

I dragged Pawnee boy off the trail and stuck him back for finding later. I can't say I was upset in a normal way. I was sure sorry Pawnee boy was dead and that Belle was off with that pack of rascals, but they'd left tracks enough to follow even in the dark of night. I wasn't fretful. I wasn't anxious. I pulled the rifle off of Gunther and checked to see if it had all the load it could hold. I did the same with my Colt. The only plan I made was something like "By God, those sons-of-bitches," and then I took Gunther's reins and followed tracks up the way.

I knew where I was, and I knew exactly who'd counseled me to get there. Him with the corset and the lipstick and the powdered eyes. It's peculiar who can end up being right in this life and why. Doctrines of demons is what he'd told us. Devil up, he'd said.

There wasn't much challenge to tracking them, I figured I'd close on that bunch in time. I didn't dawdle, but I didn't hurry. We just trudged along behind them, which gave me occasion to wonder why Belle hadn't warned us off down the trail. At length, I decided there were things in life that simply had to happen, that even a witchy girl could only put off for so long.

When I told Gunther what I was working through, he

stepped on the back of my boot because he was only ever first a mule.

That bunch looked to have killed a man and maybe his son as they'd passed through. Their bodies were barely off the trail, and one had suffered from Dupree's shotgun while the other, the father, had wounds all over and not all of them from bullets. It looked like those fellows had taken time out for some fun.

I had my shovel still, but the ground was too cold to put them in it, so I said a few words over that pair and left them where they were. The wonder of it was that Dupree and them were camped not even a mile up the trail. They must have come to think they had no cause at all to run and worry, could handle anybody who might have mustered the pluck to head their way.

I didn't grow nervous or anxious even after I'd seen their fire. It was late afternoon, so I just had light enough to account for them all. I'd left Gunther back trailside and was slipping up with both my guns when I saw Belle in among them. Dupree had her on his lap. He was being awfully familiar with her. I didn't like that much, but I kept my head and applied myself to thinking through how I would kill them.

I put the Goins brothers as one and two, since they seemed wild and ready, and then Dupree's trashy associates who appeared to be too drunk to shoot. I'd kill the one who shot me first and then the other two. I was holding Dupree to the end since all he had was that shotgun and a wicked appetite for children, as best I could tell.

So that was the scheme, and I was settling into a firm

spot with my granddaddy's Winchester where I planned
to wait on Belle to get herself out of the way. But then one
of Dupree's boys, the one Arturo had shot and who'd shot
me, pulled out his pistol and gave it to Belle. He told her
to go kill some supper with it.

"Or hell, sweetie, you can shoot me if you want?" He
howled, and the rest of them hooted.

It was all Belle could do to hold that heavy pistol off the
ground. She'd never shown an interest in guns, seemed to
have no use for shooting, but would hang back and watch
while we were dealing with scoundrels on the trail. So I
wasn't at all surprised to see her struggling with the thing,
but once she picked it up with both hands and had drawn
the hammer back, we all got a lot more interested in what
she might be up to, especially once she'd swing around to
find a Goins brother. When that gun went off, it knocked
both of them down.

I shot the other Goins before he could kill her and then
put a round in the boy who'd shot me, but I missed those
other two. They'd lit out into the woods and were busting
through the underbrush. I put a quick bullet in Dupree
before I went after the strays.

Those boys might have thought they were getting away,
but they ran in kind of a circle, and were panting and
looking behind themselves when they both came up my
way.

I was waiting with my Colt out. "Didn't have to come
to this," I said.

One of them wanted to do some pleading. I could tell
that well enough. But the other one, even drunk, thought

too much of himself to beg. He was carrying a Dragoon and had it half out of his holster by the time I'd a bullet in him and his buddy both. It didn't occur to me there might be any room for mercy. Once I'd deviled up, that wasn't a thing that came into my head.

Belle was standing by Dupree waiting for me by the time I reached the camp. He was still alive, but he wasn't going to make it. That rifle had opened him up but good, and he was suffering for it. Belle picked up his top hat and pitched it into the fire.

"They do anything to you?" I asked her.

She shook her head. She tooted.

"Do it," Dupree told me. He was twitching and gurgling by then.

I had my Colt out and ready, but I didn't pull the trigger. I knew the worst thing I could do was leave that man like he was. He'd probably hang on and suffer a while until the cold got to him, unless the wolves and the coyotes showed up first.

When he saw we were leaving him there, Dupree had something like a fit and called me everything he could come up with to try to make me kill him. Instead, we just gathered our horses and left him laying where he was.

"This ain't no way to do," he finally said like he had some kind of standards. I had no qualms about going off, didn't feel bad about him at all. I didn't feel bad about any of them. I didn't feel a thing.

We went straight back to Pawnee boy, traveled through the night to reach him, and I explained to Belle along the way why he wouldn't want a hole, so she was ready

to help me gather limbs, pile them up, and lay him on
them. I didn't feel like saying much while we watched
him burn but just wished Pawnee boy farewell and decent
luck where he was going. Then we struck out north up the
wagon road and made for Breckenridge.

That town was good for us. They had a hotel there
where we took a room and hunkered down against the
winter. About every third day we'd visit Gunther in a barn-
yard up past the mill. He didn't mind the cold. He'd stand
in the snow even when he didn't need to and nudge and
nuzzle the horses shifting around under blankets out there.

As for us, we were content enough, I guess. That was no
easy thing to tell with Belle. She tooted and snorted and
liked when I'd read from one of Arturo's books. He hadn't
given it to me. I'd just come away with it. The thing was
full of poetry, flowery stuff I could barely navigate. I'd stop
to figure out words and so get the flow all wrong, but Belle
didn't seem to mind, and I guess I didn't either. We were
usually just pleased to be back in the old days for a while.

I made a few changes while we were there, stuck in
Breckenridge. I sold my rifle to a boy. I kept my Colt but
wouldn't wear it because I'd known time to think about all
I'd gotten up to since the plains. I wasn't ashamed of any
of it. I'd been in territory where the law was something
you helped the scoundrels keep. I figured that place would
settle down. I felt like I'd done a bunch of rough business
nobody would presently be required to do.

But even if I didn't have anything like regrets, I was
afraid of what I might become if I didn't make some kind
of break before we crossed the mountains. So I let grand-

daddy's rifle go and packed away my sidearm and went around as some young fellow who was caring for a child. I told folks she was French and shy about it. We bought her better clothes, and there were women in town who were pleased to take Belle in hand and gussie her up.

They soon gave up trying to teach her English, complained to me she wouldn't even speak French. They did get her to where she could walk with a Bible balanced on her head and curtsy if they barked at her enough. They even managed to curl her hair, and Belle indulged them after a fashion. I'd let her know it was all temporary and she wouldn't have curls or books to balance after Breckenridge.

Come spring, we bought our way onto a wagon train heading west. They had guides and a pack of roughnecks who'd been hired on to keep the way clear, and they were serious and sober enough to put me at my ease. We had a small cart Gunther pulled with precious little enthusiasm. I got the feeling he was reminded of the old days pulling our cart back home. He was a different mule by then and seemed to have decided he rated better.

We didn't see any Indians or any people much until we'd crossed the desert and cleared the line down into California where we passed into gold mining territory out around Placerville. It was funny to think I'd been aiming to get there after we'd arrived, because I didn't care anything about gold anymore.

I did see a nugget finally. A fellow in the road had one he was anxious to show off. He kept it buttoned up tight in his top shirt pocket wrapped in a handkerchief, and he made a big show of putting it onto his palm where I could see it.

"Look!" he said.

I did. That was enough.

I thought at first we'd take a boat around and make our way back east, but I decided to put that off because I didn't much want to leave Gunther. So we went on west, just us, and stopped at a place called Junction City, which is Roseville now but was hardly anywhere at all back then.

I got to know a guy there who was maybe ten years older than me. He was ambitious and truly oversupplied with gumption. He had business plans of every stripe and was the sort to execute them, but he needed somebody like me to be sour on stuff and put on the brakes. He opened a store and got in and out of hotel keeping twice. He had a mortuary for a while, a fleet of wagons to carry freight, and he ran a ferry on one of the lakes until it caught fire and sank. He'd use any profit that came his way to kick off something new. I tried to help him get insolvent slower.

It was a living, and that's all that mattered to me. We didn't need much to squeak by. I built a house down south around Antelope where we could be off to ourselves, and I kept thinking I'd find time to keep some cows or plant a crop, but it was easier drawing regular pay, so that's what I stuck and stayed with while we let people around decide whatever they wanted about us. Some thought we were brother and sister. Some thought we were husband and wife. Either one was fine because we knew the actual story. I was a boy from back in the Alleghenies. Belle was a girl I'd found in a wagon. We'd had a wild time together. There wasn't much to tell past that.

She stayed who she was, tooting and sneering and failing to speak up. We took long walks together around the countryside, and she'd keep to the house while I went off to work. She planted flowers one year and messed around with a garden plot. By the next spring she'd quit all that and did a fair bit of visiting with Gunther. I'd catch her humming tunes sometimes but could never make out what they were.

Gunther went first, and it would have been sad even though he was an antique by then if he'd not laid down and died right across the front landing. He'd come out of the barn lot and over to the house, must have been feeling like he was going and wanted, being a mule, to get in the way. I was past hole digging by then, had to hire a man to do it, and it was a painful thing to watch his tractor roll old Gunther in.

I thought I'd be next, but Belle wouldn't have it. She

started getting smaller. There was never much to her, but she'd soon lost all her fat and some of her muscle. I carried her to the doctor. Back then they were left to poke and guess. He had ideas about what her complaint might be and wanted to open her up for a look, but Belle wouldn't allow it, and I didn't see fit to bring it up with her again. It seemed to me, since she was a witchy thing, she probably knew what was coming and so hardly needed a doctor to have a gawk around and say.

If she had pain, she never showed it. Her breath got short. She'd take a chair and stay in it all day. Then the bed grew inviting for her, and she would rarely leave it. One morning I went in to see her, and she just wasn't around anymore.

I arranged to have her buried in a churchyard up the road, and me and the guy I worked for stood at the graveside with the preacher. I remember thinking that Belle would finish in an especially nice hole.

She got a Psalm from the preacher. We all sang a hymn, and I told her from memory, "Behold I go where I know infinity to dwell." Then I walked home, sat on the porch for a while, and went on with living from there.

I kept on getting older than I'd ever wanted to be and quit working when my hips got balky. I took to roaming around the yard and reading magazines, looking at the pictures anyway. Once I'd fallen down a couple of times, my boss's wife took an interest in me. He was dead by then and she filled her time helping people like me out.

She came around the house with a fellow from a place up the road where old folks who'd gone unsteady lived in rooms of their own and had minders to keep them square. Nurses, that is, and orderly types who could pick them up off the floor. I resisted at first. That's my natural way, but I fell onto the sofa one evening when I was aiming just to pass it, and that left me to wonder if maybe my starch wasn't finally giving out.

So I moved up the road to see how that might go, and aside from the food and the smell of the place, it suited me all right. I had a room with a window, a bed and a dresser, and my own bathroom that a lady named Bessie cleaned for me every other day. She was all the way out from Georgia, so we talked about stuff back home.

I'd been there for a year when the college people came. That would have been October of 1956. One of them was some kind of fancy professor, and the other was his student. She was a dainty thing in a cardigan who appeared to be new to lipstick, and they spent an hour in the sunroom setting up their recording machine. It was about the size of a steamer trunk with big reels of tape and wires and knobs and glowing vacuum tubes. It didn't appear that either one of them knew exactly how to work it, but together they finally managed to get it to do what they wished.

They had a table set up with a microphone on it, and people who wanted could sit down and talk. Ordinarily, I would have been parked out on the veranda watching the road, but with those two there, I ducked into the sun room to see what they were up to and got to hear a lady rattle on about the great depression. Then some fellow talked for half an hour about fighting in World War I. He'd loaded a cannon for two years and had lost a finger at it.

Once he'd finally finished and gotten up, the professor turned to me. He pointed at the empty chair, the microphone, said, "Please."

I wasn't aware I wanted it out until I started talking because I'd held it all close and tamped down for so long.

The girl had a pad open on her lap and her pencil raised and ready. The professor pulled his glasses off so he could rub his eyes.

"1879," I said. "Along about April, I think. Just me and my mule, out there in the scrub. I believe it was Oklahoma."

They both perked up. They were pleased, I guess, I wasn't going to talk about Hoover and how we used to squeeze a nickel.

"Somewhere west of Enid," I told them, "I killed a Comanche. Twice."

Made in United States
Orlando, FL
22 March 2022